HIDER, SEEKER, SECRET KEEPER

ALSO BY ELIZABETH KIEM

Dancer, Daughter, Traitor, Spy
Orphan, Agent, Prima, Pawn

HIDER, SEEKER, SECRET KEEPER

ELIZABETH KIEM

SOHO
TEEN

Published in the United States by Soho Teen
an imprint of
Soho Press, Inc.
853 Broadway
New York, NY 10003

Library of Congress Cataloging-in-Publication Data

Kiem, Elizabeth
Hider, seeker, secret keeper / Elizabeth Kiem.
Sequel to: Dancer, daughter, traitor, spy.
ISBN 978-1-61695-569-4
eISBN 978-1-61695-413-0
[1. Mystery and detective stories. 2. Ballet dancing—Fiction. 3. Bolshoi
Ballet Company—Fiction.] I. Title.
PZ7.K54Hi 2014
[Fic]—dc23
2014009577
Interior design by Janine Agro, Soho Press, Inc.

Printed in the United States of America

10 9 8 7 6 5 4 3 2 1

Seems like nothing I said
Ever meant anything
But a headline over my head.
Thought I made a stand
Only made a scene.
There's no feast for the underfed.
All the unknown, dying or dead
Keep showing up in my dreams.
I'll shut up and carry on.
The scream becomes a yawn.

"Dreams So Real" by Metric

CAST OF CHARACTERS:

Russians use many names. In addition to first and last names, a "patronymic," derived from the father's given name, serves as a sort of middle name. Addressing a Russian by first name and patronymic (Anna Dmitrievna, Ludmila Kirilovna) is a show of respect. Addressing a close friend by any of a number of diminutive nicknames is also common.

This cast of characters is provided to help readers unfamiliar with Russian names.

MOSCOW:

Daniela Mitrokhin (also Dana)—a dancer in the corps de ballet of the Bolshoi Ballet.

Stas—A scene designer at the Bolshoi Theatre.

Lana Viktorovna Dukovskaya (also Lanochka)—a dancer in the corps de ballet of the Bolshoi Ballet.

Marina Viktorovna Dukovskaya (also Marya)—Lana's mother and a former Bolshoi ballerina.

Boris Strelets—a Trustee of the Board of the Bolshoi Ballet.

Pavel Artemovich Vartukh (also Pasha)—artistic director of the Bolshoi Ballet.

Anna Dmitrievna Arkhipova (also Anya)—former ballerina and second in command of the Bolshoi Ballet.

Ludmila Kirilovna—Lana's ballet teacher.

Arkady Grigorievich Danilov—the (former) artistic director of the Bolshoi Ballet.

Nina Oleynikova (also Ninochka, Neen)—a dancer in the corps de ballet of the Bolshoi Ballet.

NEW YORK:

Georgi Ivanovich Levshik (also Gosha)—Russian-American businessman.

Roma Buslov—Russian-American trumpet player employed by Georgi Levshik.

Benjamin Frame—Russian-American musician and music scholar.

HISTORICAL FIGURES:

Galina Ulanova—Bolshoi ballerina and *prima ballerina assoluta*, from 1944–1960.

Sergei Rachmaninov—20th century Russian pianist and composer.

Mstislav Rostropovich—20th century Russian cellist and conductor.

Igor Stravinsky—20th century Russian composer of *The Rite of Spring*.

Vaslav Nijinsky—20th century Russian dancer and choreographer of *The Rite of Spring*.

Pyotr Tchaikovsky—19th century Russian composer.

A glossary of Russian words and phrases can be found at the back of the book.

ACT ONE
THE CHOSEN ONE
MOSCOW

ONE
BLOOD DIAMOND

The night that Daniela almost died, I wanted to kill her myself.

That sounds terrible. Not because I wanted to kill my friend but because, you know, who cares what I wanted. She's the one who will never dance again.

I can actually hear her voice. I can hear her scolding: *Lana, why's it always got to be about you? Do you have to make everything personal?*

Well, no. I guess I don't. I guess I could sit by Daniela's hospital bed and hold her hand. I could meet all the suspicious glances with big, dumb eyes. I could tell myself: *this has nothing to do with you, Lana.*

But I would be wrong.

Call me a narcissist if you like, but when my friend Daniela was nearly killed—and not by me—I knew I should take it personally.

• • •

WE WERE JUST OUT on a lark, me and Stas.

I was supposed to be in repertoire class, but to hell with that. It was a warm spring day, the streets tickled with pollen and the sky blown by clouds the size of small Siberian lakes. A glorious mid-May afternoon like that and you've got no business locking yourself in a windowless practice room. Not when you've poured your soul into windowless practice for four months, only to find out you've been passed over.

We're sending Daniela on the New York tour. She's the more reliable dancer.

I could have accepted the decision graciously and headed back into the studio: that place where I had given it my all and stayed late every night. That place full of edgy egos, shifting alliances, and the occasional unwanted advance from our playboy of an artistic director, Pavel Vartukh. That place where I had maybe thrown one or two tantrums—not because I'm a diva, but because I don't react well to abuse. And trust me, the rehearsal studio where the New York tour was being assigned was a den of abuse—abuse of power, talent, and aspiration.

So I didn't head back for more. I figured I was in Moscow, and I was staying in Moscow. The sun dappled the city like a chandelier. It was half empty, the traffic drained from the center out Rublevskoye highway, west to the mega-*dachas* and the "rustic" shopping malls where the wealthy people summer behind electric gates.

Stas wanted to head that way, too. Out Rublevskoye. A box holder—one of those odious types who brings their own booze to the Bolshoi performances and has an entourage waiting backstage during intermission—was throwing a party at his country estate. I said I wouldn't be caught dead at a party like that. Anybody with enough money for season tickets to the Bolshoi Ballet is automatically disqualified from my list of respectable fans. Anybody who calls his *dacha* a "country estate" is a grade-A douchebag. This guy Strelets, in particular, is a perv as well as a philistine.

But he is powerful. He can make or break a dancer who graces the gardens of his country estate.

I tried shaming Stas, reminding him how Strelets had once painted testicles on *The Nutcracker*'s grandfather clock. I figured that as a set designer, Stas would be more outraged by that insult than the ones regularly endured by us ballerinas. But he just laughed and tried a new tactic.

"If I take the back way through Dmitrovka, we can fly. There won't be any traffic on those narrow roads. Six minutes and we'll be out of town. Top velocity."

He saw me waver. I'm a speed demon. He handed me the spare helmet.

"C'mon Lana. It's Friday night," he wheedled. "We don't have to stay long. Just long enough for you to charm Mr. Box Holder into weighing in on your behalf. What you do is you feed him strawberries and sniffle sadly. Tomorrow he'll call the theater, indignant that you've been robbed of your place on the tour."

"How'd you know?" I asked.

"Could see it on your face. They made New York assignments yesterday, right?"

I nodded. I thought about my face. What exactly did it show? I'm not a sullen girl, not prone to sniffles.

"Let's see your pout," teased Stas.

"Cute," I said. "You're real cute." My heart was heavy, though.

ONCE UPON A TIME, when the Bolshoi Ballet was the most prestigious in the world, hard work and talent would get you to the stage and something deep and indefinable would make you beloved—an "Artist of the People," a hero in feathers and tulle. But that was long ago, before the Bolshoi became a victim of the same crass commerce and greed that have spoiled the only things about the old Soviet Union that were worth any pride.

Here's a quick history lesson, courtesy of a girl more interested in flexibility than ideology, better at *pas de bourrée* than politics: Thirty years after the collapse of Communism, Russia is both richer and poorer than it was back then, and nowhere is that contradiction more on display than at the Bolshoi Theatre. Because the only thing as steady as the money pumped into the theater are the scandals that come skulking out its back door. Sordid headlines about the truth behind the Bolshoi's curtains are regular tabloid fare: embezzlement, bribery, corruption, vendettas.

Sure, a lot of it is sensational nonsense—like the story about Pavel Vartukh's secret gay lover who came back from a sex-change operation in Belgrade ready to become a prima ballerina. I mean—what? But too much of it is based in the truth that we all recognize: Fortune has trumped fame. Greed has bested grace. Put simply, starring roles at the ballet are more easily bought than earned.

Which is why Stas and his pep talk failed to cheer me up.

I GRABBED THE HELMET from Stas. Swung it around like it was my wrecking ball.

Daniela may be the more reliable dancer, but I am the better dancer. I wanted to believe that the day would come again when that was the only consideration for a Bolshoi ballerina. Or that, more realistically, a day might come when pigs like Strelets still ordered around goats like Vartukh, but girls like Daniela and me could be left alone to dance hard, but in peace.

"Okay, listen," I told Stas. "I will go and I will take a swim in the pool, and I will drink two glasses of wine: one to Daniela's success and one to our corpulent host's imminent cardiac arrest. And then we leave. Got it?"

Stas smiled. Maybe he thought that, deep down, I wanted to go to this party to work my advantage. I would let him believe it. Not because it was true. But because the only thing more humiliating than being a suck-up to a powerful "friend" of the Bolshoi Ballet is being afraid of one. Keeping your distance is one thing. Hiding your head in the sand is another.

I added, "But if that nasty toad Strelets gets too close I want you to shout: 'There's not a man here who can shoot a bigger gun than me!'"

"How about: 'There's not a man here who can piss farther than me!'" Stas suggested.

"No—better: 'There's not a man here who can put more ballerina toes in his mouth than me!'"

"Got it," said Stas. "That will certainly divert his attention."

He looked down at my feet. "Good girl. Motorcycle boots. Excellent for joyrides and discouraging foot fetishes alike."

The instant he hit the gas, I felt my disappointment slip away. We turned onto the tree-lined boulevard, and the pale green necklace of Moscow's inner ring worked with me. I stretched out my hand and gave the early leaves a high five. Then I squeezed Stas. I needed some speed in my budding spring. He obliged with a rev of his engine and a reckless dodge in the slow lane.

Downhill from the raucous geometry and bright paint of Saint Basil's Cathedral, we encountered the Friday evening traffic. The Kremlin, seat of State power loomed above us, the sun sparking its gold, and we raced along the Moscow River's floodplain, headed west. We crossed the river on an old bridge, crossed it again on an older one, and then we were scattering roadside crows disoriented by the lengthening days.

Once Moscow was behind us, it felt as if we were in another era. At least to me. An era when Moscow stopped after three concentric rings around the Kremlin. I closed my eyes and wished that the road would never end, or that when it did, it would end at a lopsided wooden *dacha* with wide verandahs and hand-carved windowsills. A place where wealth was measured in books. Or letters. Or best . . . acres of woods and fields.

Stas turned left and then right and we joined the inching parade of weekenders. We hadn't really left Moscow after all. Just made a ruckus down her underarm and got caught in her fist. We weaved in and out of gridlock, our reflections everywhere. There are a lot of tinted windows on the Rublevskoye highway. We arrived in their hot mess.

The guard outside the high metal gates checked me out. In my jeans, boots and helmet I didn't exactly exude *ballerina*. But Stas dropped the right name and the guard nodded. As he opened the gates to let us pass, I could feel him searching me for my supple, slender calling card.

Sorry chump, I thought. *I left my wings and tiara backstage tonight.*

Boris Strelets, president of Krylatskoye Bank, trustee of the Bolshoi Ballet and member of the parliamentary committee on cultural investment, was walking his greyhounds down the driveway as we pulled in. He wore tight black jeans that looked terrifically uncomfortable. He reminded me of whatever you call a squirmy, slow thing. Fifteen years ago he was almost certainly a grub. But now, with his wealth and his government connections and his new artistic pet project—the ballet—he was a *vazhnaya persona*: a VIP, a person of significance.

I groaned. Stas was already striding toward our host, his hand outstretched. Strelets looked up, clearly hoping to see a young woman instead. I sidestepped into a grove of palm trees. Grateful, by God, for fake imported landscaping where once upon a time there must have been gooseberry bushes. I heard the crackle of a sound system on overdrive. Then the cackle of Julia Zemphira, the most coveted dance DJ in Moscow.

"*Rebyata—kakaya okhuitel'naya vecherinka!*"

Oh yes, Julia. A freaktastic evening indeed.

I was already sick of this party. And it wasn't even dark yet.

LOOK. I GAVE IT my best shot. I drank the wine and I swam in the pool. I even accepted a fluffy robe from one of Strelets's associates who had scooped up my dry clothes and refused to give them back until I danced with him. "Sure I'll dance with you," I said, and then I hitched up the robe and did thirty *fouetté* turns in a circle around him while he tried to groove to Rihanna. Okay, that was a little arrogant, I'll grant you. Larisa sneered at me: *Showy bitch*. But Galya applauded. And Galya, as a soloist, is better billed than Larisa, for the record. At any rate, I got my clothes back and the guy moved on to more pleasant partners.

After an hour I was done. Done with the overly loud laughter, the bad pop music, the manic staccato of *New York, New York, New York*, like crickets from every corner. I had avoided a fight, avoided a proposition; the evening was as close as it could be to a success.

I found Stas in the billiard room, holding his own with two tight-lipped millionaires and a handful of drunk dancers who thought it terribly funny to snatch the billiard balls from the table before they dropped in the pockets.

"As soon as this game's over, K?" he whispered in acknowledgment. "I think I got these guys."

I was just about to point out that the game was not going to end as long as the ball-plucker brigade held court when I was cut short by the mean crack of wood and the languid roll of an imperfect bank shot. The giggling dancers fell silent. One of the men—an oil executive maybe, or maybe that guy who owns all the foreign car dealerships—stood frozen. My eyes followed the cue to its tip. To the splayed white hand trapped under it. Up the thin wrist and tapered arm to the soft shoulder topped by a face flickering with shock and pain. Tatiana Ribakova bit her lip and, after an endless moment, let out a small wounded protest.

"Touch my balls once more, my pigeon . . ." hissed the man. And then one of the ugliest threats I have ever heard out of the mouth of one of our Bolshoi patrons. I wondered if the man had ever seen a swan with a broken wing.

Stas stepped in and handled it. Soon Tatiana had her hand in an ice bucket and the offended billiard player had an iced bottle in his. By the time we made our exit, Tatiana was pleading for forgiveness: "*Nu, Vasya* . . . please, sweetheart, it was just in fun. Did you have money on it? Because you know I can make it up to you. You know I'm your balls' biggest fan."

So you see what I'm saying, here? I was sick to my stomach when we left. But it still wasn't over.

Because as we made our way back to the city, dusk trailing us like a cape, we saw them: Daniela and Vartukh.

They were at one of those roadside shopping strips that sell sushi, sauvignon blanc and hothouse roses. Daniela had a bouquet in her arms; Pavel Vartukh had Daniela's waist in his. I thought I saw discomfort flash across my friend's face. A visceral reaction to bodies out of alignment. This, after all, was not rehearsal. This was Friday night on Rublevskoye highway. This was the artistic director of the Bolshoi Ballet in a very public display of close relations with a junior dancer who until one month ago was still a minor. Not that it was a first. Not for Pavel Vartukh. For Daniela, maybe. But not for Vartukh.

I tapped Stas on the shoulder and he nodded. He saw, too. He knew what it meant that Daniela was going to New York and now was in Vartukh's arms. Once upon a time, Stas and Daniela were a thing, and even though that ended a while ago, he's probably a better friend to her than I am. That's just how it is. Stas is an ex; I am a rival.

I mean, I thought we were more than that. I thought we were two-thirds of a tight triangle—me, Daniela and Nina. A confident threesome that, I suppose, had not yet had our confidence tested. We were the closest friends you could find in the theater, I'd wager.

But the bottom line? No friendship at the Bolshoi outweighs ambition.

I know that now. I knew it the moment I saw Daniela on Vartukh's arm. Saw her glance up at the sound of Stas's bike. Saw her toss her head in fake laughter and turn her back to the road.

With that, she broke my heart harder than she ever hurt Stas.

"Run them down?" he asked over his shoulder.

"With glee," I said.

Stas lowered his visor, revved his engine and we leaped toward the shallow pull-off like it was dinner. We were not more than ten meters from them when I panicked and gripped his forearm, just where a partner would touch to signal a turn. But Stas had already adjusted, and with a squeal we swerved into a service road parallel to the highway and sped past the tarted-up sushi lounge. Stas stopped at the next traffic light, though it was only just yellow. We didn't say a word. We didn't say a word all the way into town, and Stas drove at a respectable speed.

Then I was home, lying on the couch watching a bad crime series on TV. I had purged my nausea and ignored my heartsick. But I felt this residue. These freaked-out goosebumps like a light sheen of mental sweat. Like I had had a close call.

Not that any of it had anything to do with me, mind you.

THAT WAS THREE NIGHTS ago. A million years ago. And now I am at Daniela's bedside, holding her hand. I'm wishing she would say it: *Lana, why's it always got to be about you? This has nothing to do with you.* But Daniela's not talking. Not yet. The motorcycle that ran her down outside that sushi bar (a BMW, say the investigators) broke her back and ruined her face on the asphalt. The doctors say that she will recover. In time she will walk, they say. But dancing? Not likely. Not ever.

My phone rings. It's my mother.

It was she who delivered the news that night, waking me from a deep sleep on the couch to tell me that Vartukh and Daniela were both in the hospital. At first, it didn't register—the part about "hit-and-run." It sounded like some sort of new choreography I hadn't learned, that's how groggy I was from too-early sleep. But the more she talked, the more I prayed I was still asleep and in the middle of a bad dream.

"Imagine—a motorcyclist! There's no way you can jump the curb on a motorcycle, hit two people and not even know it," she had said. "It must have been intentional. Imagine—someone deliberately ran them down. On a motorcycle."

My mother has a gift for stating the obvious.

I have that gift, too. But for me it has mostly been a curse. Like when I told a journalist that I thought most of the money for the Bolshoi Theatre's billion-dollar renovation went to PR pockets and to publicity campaigns about the Bolshoi Theatre's billion-dollar renovation. Or when I told my teacher, Ludmila Kirilovna, that she showed more interest in her annual ticket allotment (which brought in more than twice her salary on the scalper's market) than in her students' training. Or when I told Vartukh himself that he's a misogynist. Or when I announced to the entire cafeteria that if they put *Spartacus* on the spring schedule again I would organize a boycott against bare-chested ballets.

"*Pochemu s toboy vsegda skandaly?*" my mother asks. Why must you always make a scene?

I don't have an answer. I can see pretty clearly where my loud mouth has gotten me: third-tier status and a world of suspicion. But I can't help it. It's hard for me to bite my tongue. Maybe it's because my mother can. And does. My mother's the champ of keeping quiet. Oh, the untold injustices that she has silently endured, Marina Dukovskaya. And I say untold because, well, she's never told me about them. She states the obvious, sure. But she won't say a word about the secrets. And she has many. My mother, Marina Dukovskaya, is a cipher. A riddle. A mystery she refuses to help me solve.

I step away from Daniela's bed and answer the call.

"*Da, Mama . . .*"

"Lana. They are looking for you at the theater. Anna Arkhipova just called."

"What did she want?"

"I don't know. But it worried me, Lana. She mentioned Friday. She said you skipped class. I covered for you. I said you were with me. At Novodevichy Cemetery. It was the Feast of Bright Friday, Lana."

"Are you insane?" I ask. But it sounds like a statement. "Are. You. Insane. 'Cover for me?' That's what you said, Ma, that you 'covered for me'? What's that? You suspect me, too?"

"I didn't say that. I used the wrong word."

I can hear defense lock elbows in my mother's voice.

"I meant that you need a better alibi. It looks bad."

"Of course it looks bad, Ma. Because no matter where

I was Friday during class, everyone at Boris Strelets's place saw me leaving there Friday night. Leaving, as a matter of fact, around nine P.M. On Stas's motorcycle. Looking bad."

There's a long silence. Neither of us can think of something more obvious to say.

"Bright Friday, Ma? I don't even know what that is."

"Something to do with a virgin mother. A life-giving spring. Some old icon," she mumbles. I can hear her twisting the phone cord.

"And Novodevichy?" I ask eventually. "We don't even have family in Novodevichy Cemetery."

"Everyone has family in Novodevichy," says my mother.

I lift a dusty slat in the plastic blind. From Daniela's hospital room I can see the golden domes of the Novodevichy Convent. I don't bother to ask. Who, among the tortured artists laid to rest under the crenellated, white-washed walls of Novodevichy, does my mother consider family? Does she mean Galina Ulanova, Joseph Stalin's pet ballerina? Or the renowned cellist, Rostropovich? Is it the novelist who threw his unfinished masterpiece in the flames rather than die the author of an unfinished masterpiece? The poet who figured suicide was better than censorship?

I'm not surprised that my mother, a woman who left Russia for America and buried her father there before returning to her homeland to dance, feels a kinship with the legends lying deep under carpets of pine needles. They are resting even deeper in the false nostalgia of

Marina's generation. The Soviet Union's last youth—disenchanted, disassociated and orphaned (in my mother's case, literally) by a swift current of change.

Still, it galls me that she could say something like that: "everyone has family," when I, in fact, don't. I have only Marina and her secrets. She might as well be the virgin mother of Bright Friday for all I know about her past.

"How is she? Daniela?" she asks.

"Still unconscious. She looks dreadful. They really messed her up, Ma."

I turn and look again at Daniela's bruised face. Her eyes are slits of pain. There are lacerations down her neck and a terrible burn on her left cheek.

"But Vartukh is already discharged," I say. "Nothing but a dislocated shoulder."

My mother mumbles platitudes: "Thank God for that."

I wonder. It seems unlikely that God had much to do with it. Daniela is maimed, and Pavel Vartukh, artistic director and serial womanizer, will wave at the paparazzi and go back to work. That doesn't strike me as divine will.

"Let's talk when I get home, Ma, okay?"

"Please don't be late," she says, her voice a whisper.

I hang up the phone and close the blind. Then I move back to the bed and lean over my friend's disfigured face.

"Daniela, I'll be back tomorrow. I'll be back with Nina. So try to make yourself presentable, girlfriend."

I grab her hand and squeeze it tightly. *"Derzhis'."* Hang on.

• • •

IT'S A LONG WALK from the hospital to the Bolshoi
Theatre, but the sun is out and it feels healing, antisep-
tic. Still, every step of the way I am replaying the events
of 72 hours ago.

I think again of the pain I felt when Anna Arkhipova,
Vartukh's mouthpiece, delivered the verdict: *Daniela is
the more reliable dancer.* And there was more—Nina
had been chosen as the tour understudy for the corps.
Our threesome divided, and I'm the odd girl out.

It hurts. But not just because I was passed over. That's
not why I am angry. This is something else. It hurts
because I suspect that Daniela sold me out.

It's not a secret—me and my issues with the Bolshoi.
I'm the one who speaks too loudly about the theater's
fat budget and fatter trustees; its gilded face, bloated
guts, moldering foundation. I'm the one who questions
the star billing and the ticket mafia. But I know the others agree. Daniela did. As often as she admonished my
outbursts, she still had my back. *Lana's gonna run this
show one day*, she sometimes joked.

Look, I knew we were in direct competition—that is
as natural a stance for a ballerina as first position. But
I thought that we were both flirting with another possi-
bility—that we could be partners. We could be pioneers.
Plenty of our best dancers have defected—to Covent Gar-
den, to Berlin, to American Ballet Theatre in New York.
We could be the first to leave the Bolshoi without leaving home. We could join a new, independent dance troupe

here in Moscow. A clean slate, a clean stage. With no dirty money. And no baggage. No Vartukh. No *Spartacus*.

"We could dance to music from the twenty-first century!" Daniela used to cry.

"Goodbye limp dicks and hardened arteries!" I would cheer.

We even brought Ninochka in on it, dropping hints, feeling her out. And she surprised us both by saying she had already had a few exchanges with the director of Dolgorukov, a four-year-old company that got excellent reviews last year for its *a cappella* ballet *Vox Pop*. We went together, the three of us, to a few other recitals—small theater affairs—and we tried to convince ourselves that we didn't need union representation or dressing rooms with heated floors.

I thought, *Maybe this could happen.*

Sort of.

Because assignments for the Bolshoi tour to New York were also happening.

I don't mean I expected Daniela or Nina to turn down the opportunity to go to New York. Of course not. I certainly wouldn't, in their position. But there was something about the way she turned her back. The way she turned her face up to Vartukh's. The way I could feel all the way across the lanes of self-absorbed traffic a whisper campaign starring Daniela Mitrokhin with Pavel Vartukh as her confessor: *You do know, don't you, that Lana Dukovskaya is arranging meetings with Dolgorukov? I'm not even sure she could find time in her schedule to accompany the corps to New York.*

That's why I wanted to kill her. Because I thought she had chosen to play their game, and I took her about-face personally.

But I didn't want to admit that to my mother. Because Marina would be the first to agree. It's one thing for me to gripe. But it's another thing to have it confirmed by my mother, a faded star of the ballet: *The Bolshoi was once our crown jewel. Now it's a blood diamond.*

TWO
DANSE SACRALE

It's hard to recognize the accomplished ballerina that Anna Dmitrievna Arkhipova once was. That is, it's hard to recognize the dancer; the success is every bit as bright as her platinum hair, as outlined as her fuchsia lips and scapular brows, as enhanced as . . . well, everything in Arkhipova's well-appointed office in the Bolshoi Theatre.

She has me wait, as always, outside in the corridor with the picture windows looking over Theatre Square. I take in the view, peeling back the years to imagine how it must have looked to my mother from this window when she was my age.

Back then Moscow was beautiful, but beat down. Like a girl with good bones who couldn't afford to flaunt them. Back then, the Kremlin crouched behind its wall. The ancient markets were strangers to modern marketing. No billboards, no heat lamps, no tasteful lighting or piped-in music along the passageways full of Gucci and Bulgari and Yves Saint Laurent. In the 20th century, you had to be a ballerina with dollars to buy a pair of Levi's. You had to be a commissar to park your black car on the square. Not just a dude with an Escalade.

Anna would remember that view, too. She and my mother came out of the same Academy class. Then they took very different paths. Today Anna Dmitrievna is number two in command of the ballet, while my mother barely makes ends meet, teaching girls who will never dance past the age of fifteen. Still, it's somehow easier to imagine Marina as the radiant star. Probably just because Anna has a face that looks like it would promptly melt under the stage lights.

"So, you have seen Daniela?" she asks once I am seated across from her. "Poor darling. What a tragedy. An absolute tragedy. And I can only hope and pray that her misadventure does not bring even more tragedy in tow. I spoke to your mother today."

"Yes, Anna Dmitrievna, she told me. And I would like to explain, personally, my actions last Friday." I'm ready to give a full statement, a formal disavowal of my mother's panicky alibi, but Anna puts an expensively manicured halt to my testimony.

"Your mother is overexcited," she says. "Of course. All mothers would be and yours, *nu* . . . let's just say that I welcome her involvement. We have waited a long time."

There's the barb. The refrain that Anna so often sings when the conversation turns to my mother, who, after all, "quit the Bolshoi not once, but twice!"

That's right. She skipped out first before she had even graduated the Academy. Up and moved to America at a time when that could only mean two things: you were a traitor or a spy.

"Even more dramatically, she came *back*," Anna would hoot. "I mean there we were, working our tushes off just to keep a roof over our head during that whole nightmare of 'reform' and 'rebuilding.' And for what? For the whole damn country just to collapse anyway. But we kept the box office running and the house was always full—the public, they were so grateful that we kept dancing, without salaries, without heat sometimes! And then here comes Marina Dukovskaya, fresh from New York in her pretty American leotards and custom shoes."

This is where Anna always finished her feigned delight with a superior smirk: "Well. Who would have thought?"

But not today. Today Anna doesn't dwell on my mother, who is like a specter hovering in the wings, waiting for another mistimed entry.

"Lana, you are replacing Daniela on the New York tour."

I'm uncharacteristically speechless.

"Lana. Wake up, Lana. This is real. Could I get an acknowledgment?"

Acknowledgment, yes. She wants an acknowledgment, not an apology.

"Anna Dmitrievna, thank you so much," I manage. "My mind just wasn't there. I mean I just came from the hospital and . . ."

I know I need to start at the beginning. Confirm each step that led to this unexpected turn of events.

"So, the tour has not been canceled? Because of the . . . accident?"

Anna expresses surprise like a French philosopher, flapping her lips and blowing out her cheeks. An affected gesture. And not very attractive. She knows it and recovers.

"Lana. *Chto ty?* Of course the tour goes on. Do you have any idea of the expense behind such an operation? The corporate sponsorship involved? The Metropolitan Opera House is booked for five days. It's a three-million-dollar commitment. This tragedy has no impact whatsoever on the Bolshoi's international engagement. Pavel Vartukh, as you know, sustained minor injuries—nothing graver than a dancer should expect once or twice in a career."

There it is again. The reminder. That the bottom line is the bottom line. The bottom line is money. I watch her smooth her skirt, glance sideways at her reflection in the blackened computer monitor. I try, once more, to imagine Anna Arkhipova as an idol of the stage, a woman with adoring fans instead of demanding finances. But it is impossible. Instead, I feel again that sudden shock of relief for my mother. *There but for the grace of God . . .*

"Of course," I say. "You are right, of course. Vartukh has certainly overcome greater challenges. But Daniela . . ."

I stop, mostly because Arkhipova's eyes are so ice cold. It's a nonstarter. Daniela is immaterial.

"I thought that Nina would replace Daniela in the corps," I say, still thinking I've misunderstood.

She waits a beat, watching me squirm, and then says: "For the bulk of the program, yes. Nina will replace Daniela in the corps for *Les Sylphides*, for example. But we have made some changes to the program. An addition."

Anna Dmitrievna laces her fingers together and rests them on the desk. How do these gestures become so stereotypical? Did she have to practice them? Train her fingers to express management rather than grace?

"We are considering including a small selection of interpretive excerpts. Not for every performance. One or two matinees only. We had planned for Daniela to perform the Danse Sacrale from *The Rite of Spring*."

I consider this. The Danse Sacrale. A rigorous, exercised solo from the most avant-garde of the modern ballets. Why would they give it to a junior? Why would they give it to me?

"A brilliant concept, I think," continues Anna. "I have been encouraging Vartukh for some time now. I have long thought that it's absurd to see a veteran soloist dance the Sacrale. After all, it's meant to be the Chosen One dancing for her elders, is it not? And we know perfectly well that in pagan rituals, the Chosen One would have been a maiden—a virgin."

There is so much wrong with what's she's saying that I don't know where to start.

"In the symbolic sense," Anna adds, seeing my expression. "We know you are a modern girl, Lana. But we want your youth. Your untested quality. In truth, we want your spark. Even—and I never thought I would say it—your tattoo!"

She offers a conspiratorial chuckle. I rub the miniature spotlight inside the crook of my arm. Such a tiny precision of ink that most people mistake it for a birthmark. The first tattoo to ever make it through the Bolshoi. The smallest tattoo ever to make it out of my friend Nik's parlor.

But I'm unnerved. The Danse Sacrale is legendary, yes. It's a wonderful opportunity. But the Chosen One? The one selected to dance for her elders? She's meant to dance to her death. It is not merely a sacred dance. It is a sacrificial dance. And this has not escaped me—that Daniela was chosen for a sacrificial dance. That I am the next chosen one.

There is piano music rising from the floor below. A breeze blowing through the window. Spring. In an instant my wariness is gone. Call me a pagan, but I'm suddenly utterly tuned in to the mystical sensation that there is rebirth and there is ritual, there is strife and there is sacrifice. And as long as piano music floats freely through the Bolshoi Theatre, they can all have a home here.

"*Nu, devushka*, this is your cue to accept graciously and go find a rehearsal room," says Anna. "Or have I miscalculated you?"

I am about to answer but Anna is leaning forward now. Her blouse is open against her cleavage and I see a flush of red against her breastbone. I hear the rash spread to her voice. "Your mother will be heartbroken if you miss this opportunity, Lana. If I tell her that I don't for a minute believe that you were in Novodevichy Cemetery last Friday."

I drop my eyes from her ice-cold gaze. Anna Arkhipova might not know my mother's heart, but she's got me pegged.

I am going to New York as the Chosen One.

Which means it's not really my choice after all, is it?

EIGHT DAYS IS NOT much time to learn the Danse Sacrale. Even if it is a repetitive piece. All rhythm and energy. The dance of a girl desperate to please. Arkhipova had said I could tap Masha Smirnova as a trainer, but I've seen her rendition of desperate. I don't do that sort of desperate. I have already decided that my Chosen One will dance to her death because there's nothing worth living for. Not once she's done dancing.

I find an empty rehearsal room and a scratched CD of Igor Stravinsky's *The Rite of Spring*. A hundred years old and the music is still a surprise. The first bars are lovely—reminiscent of some romance by Debussy or Chopin. Something about a faun, or a sheep, or a girl with flaxen hair. And then—goodbye to all that. The faun, the sheep and the girl with flaxen hair are driven away with taunts, ridiculed by bassoons and oboes and a single bullying alto flute.

I tie on my shoes to defend them, these quiet, slight creatures.

I spring to my toes and turn in tight propulsion to the window. I throw it open to catch the breeze and pull the blind down to keep out the light. My *Rite* will be in twilight. I pronounce it so, spread-eagle before the unseeing window. This is the position of my Chosen One: arms raised to the heavens, legs seismically braced, back turned to the audience in a silent dare—*Where will you stab me, you cowards?*

The music turns militant. The elders are demanding that the anarchy of falling night be brought under control. I give the orchestra two measures and then I join its splintered shouts for obedience. The strings are racing, tasked with starting a fire. I hear them rubbing, rubbing, looking for a spark. I stretch higher and expose my smooth surfaces—the arc of my torso, the softness under my arms, the valleys between my ribs, the long stripped trunk of my back—here's my friction for those frantic strings. I turn again, in the smallest, tightest circles, smoke rising from my toes. I leap to catch the embers sent flying from the piccolo. My arms are fans breathing life, energy, air across the dissonant heat. I set the room on fire.

A pause in the music asks me to stretch. I prepare my legs for the next sprint, my arms for the coming crucifix. I force patience. I won't decide yet how to respond to this music that is my fuel and my foe. I might embrace it. I might seduce it, confuse it. Or . . . I might slay it. Yes. I like that much better. Better than accepting that this music should kill me, the Chosen One.

The Rite of Spring is only a half hour in length. The Danse Sacrale, my sacrificial solo, is just four minutes long. By the time it arrives—the last four minutes of the ballet—I have crossed a boundary. I may have been chosen, but I will choose my own end.

Of course, this dance is not just about me. I'm perfectly aware that it's about Stravinsky, our first modern composer, and about Nijinsky, our most fearless choreographer, and about the strange rites of us God-fearing, blasphemous creatures—Russians. But when the music ends and I am covered in the kiss of sweat vanishing from my skin, *The Rite of Spring* is all about me.

WHEN I RAISE THE blinds again, the sun is resting on top of the Kremlin's tallest bell tower. I'm pleased with what I've done and I want to share it with Marina. I promised her I would not be late. Time to head home.

On the stairs I glance over the railing and see familiar freckled shoulders crowned by an auburn bun—Nina. I hesitate. I haven't spoken with her since yesterday, when she just blubbered the entire time about Daniela and Pasha. *Pasha?* I had thought. *Now Pavel, 'Vartukh the fartukh,' was 'Pasha'? How quickly we warm to the jackasses when they take a fall.*

I call down to her. She lifts her cupid face. I see relief register and she runs quickly up one flight to hug me.

"I know I should have gone but I just couldn't get the nerve," she says. "How is she? Is she better? Does she look awful? I sent flowers—did you see the flowers? I know I should have gone but . . ."

"Nina, we'll go tomorrow," I say. "She'll be better tomorrow."

Nina nods. She hugs her elbows. We never had a

chance to talk about the tour and I can see that she wants to now. I'm glad that she won't have to feel guilty anymore, about me being left out. I want her not to worry about that, so I beat her to the punch.

"Ninochka. We're going to New York. We're going to dance for Daniela, okay? That's what we'll do."

I guessed wrong. Nina is confused. "I thought that . . ."

"I just came from Arkhipova's office. It turns out that they are adding a variation. One that Dana was to perform. It's for a junior."

Nina's mouth opens, just slightly. Like she might be nauseated. Like she needs more air.

"You will dance all of *Sylphides*," I say quickly. "But I'm going, too. It's only a few performances, but I'll be there, too. You won't go alone."

"What variation?" she asks quietly.

"Danse Sacrale."

"*The Rite of Spring*?"

I nod. Nina nods. She lifts her chin, closes her mouth with a snap.

Oh please, Nina, be my ally. Be my partner.

"I've never danced it, Ninochka. I don't even know it."

I see many emotions cross her pretty face. None of them are anger—but I can see the traces of a suspicion that she doesn't even feel yet. Is it my imagination? Or is this shadow of doubt on every face I see? Including my own mother's.

Nina reaches out and grasps my hand. "You'll be amazing," she says. "Call me tomorrow and we can meet to go to the hospital." She's halfway down the steps when she stops and looks back up at me. "Congratulations."

I'M ALREADY OUT ON the street when Stas calls.

"So they brought me in. And I told them what we agreed. We didn't see them on the highway. We were home in Moscow by nine thirty."

"Stas, I'll tell them whatever you tell me to. I'll back everything you say—but I don't think anyone really cares. I mean, I don't know. I came in expecting to have to defend myself, but instead . . ."

"Instead what?" I hear his impatience. Stas is worried, guilty.

"She's still unconscious by the way," I say. "Daniela. We're going to see her tomorrow, me and Nina."

"Okay, sure," he says. "But you need to watch your back, too, Lana. I have a bad feeling. Like it's, I don't know. It's just such a weird coincidence."

"I'm thinking of selling my bike," he says a minute later.

"That's absurd."

"Maybe."

"Plus, it would look bad."

"I guess."

"Listen, I have to go. This is going to sound really strange, but I just found out that I'm going to New York."

More silence.

"Stas, did you hear me?"

"Yeah. That's just . . . a strange coincidence."

He doesn't say what we're both thinking: *and it looks bad.*

"Well. That's . . . that's great. So I'll see you tomorrow."

Stas hangs up. It feels like he hangs up on me. It feels, impossibly, like Stas suspects me as well.

IT'S NOT EVEN TEN when I get home, but Marina is already in bed.

I tiptoe into her room to turn off the light she's left burning. Her book is pinioned on the opposite pillow, her reading glasses perched on its spine. I've seen this pose many times. My fingers are on the switch when she stirs.

"You're home."

"Uh-huh."

I feel the cool pain of the double-edged sword that is my mother. I had been so excited to tell her. About the tour, about the Danse Sacrale, about being picked to solo in New York City. But now my excitement is sapped by concern. It's always like this. Something about my following in her footsteps is a threat to her. Like I'm not just her successor, I am her hunter. Suddenly the news is qualified. It's still good news, but there will be a crease in her forehead that tells me there's also bad.

"Should I turn this off?" I ask, reaching for the lamp.

"No."

She sits up, rubs her eyes, props a pillow behind her back.

"Tell me," she says.

I sigh and run my fingers through my hair. It's about three inches long—a little longer on top than in back, but not much. Running my fingers through it is like scratching an emotional itch. "I'm going. To New York. In Daniela's place."

The reaction is too subtle to gauge. But it ends in a smile. "Well, this must be the silver lining," she says.

"And they've given me a solo. From *The Rite of Spring*."

She sits forward like she's ready to bolt. Then she leans back. Exhales. Rakes her fingers across her forehead and through her own hair, still long and dark, but streaked with silver. I sit down next to her. She wriggles away to make room, knocking her book and glasses to the floor.

"Lana, it's a great honor to be chosen for a solo. But why not here? On your home stage? Why do you have to go all the way to New York for your debut? I just . . . I wish I could go with you."

"That's sweet. But it's not happening."

Her jaw tenses. Her brow knits. I bend my head and now she runs her fingers through her daughter's hair. I luxuriate in the primal feeling. It has the same effect on both of us. Which, I realize, not many things do. I'm feeling gracious. I am going to solo in New York City, I can afford to be kind. I should humor my mother. I should make this *our* triumph. Not mine.

"I have a right to intercede, you know. I'm still your mother. And I still have more experience with those people than you do."

"Okay, Ma. But I'm not sure you know Anna Dmitrievna as well as you think you do."

She scoffs. "I don't pretend to know her at all. She's the one who is always implying we have some sort of history. That we're locked in some sort of zero-sum game that started when we were children. She's the one who has decided that her success has to come at my expense. And that my happiness . . . well. I don't pretend to know Anna. But I know that she's calculated her best interests and I don't like her math."

I pull my feet up on the bed and curl closer so she can use both hands on my head. After a moment she says: "I've kept my distance. I know that it's your turn. But Lana, I have too many scars to not feel phantom pain."

More cryptic talk. I wait, not moving. I will her, silently, to tell me what, exactly, she is talking about. I give her five seconds and then conclude what I always conclude. My mother is an overly dramatic, damaged former ballerina. And she can't figure out if I will heal her or hurt her.

"Anna said your participation was 'welcome,'" I say, wondering if that was the word she used.

My mother's fingers stop.

"Anna is a manipulative shrew."

"Of course she is, Ma. That's how you get to be second in command."

Marina leans over and flips on the radio.

"The latest spectacle from the legendary Bolshoi Ballet . . . this one apparently a vendetta of sorts directed against Pavel Vartukh, the forty-seven-year-old artistic director . . . but sadly, the victim in this escapade is

an even younger member of the ballet, eighteen-year-old Daniela Mitrokhin, apparently selected for her first international tour with the ballet, but, sadly . . . her future as uncertain now as that of the troubled theater itself."

It's no accident Ma turned on the radio; we've landed in the middle of the skewer-the-Bolshoi hour. Talking head number two agrees with the radio host:

"Indeed, yes—and Pavel Vartukh is a controversial director. There are those who applaud the way he has stuck with the classic repertoire, but there seems to be so much discontent behind the scenes. So many high-profile defections from the ranks, not to mention the allegations of managerial misconduct. Naturally, this being the Bolshoi, there is no shortage of personal and powerful influences to consider . . . the comments from the office of Anna Arkhipova, who is effectively the mouthpiece of the ballet, are always informative. Her support for Vartukh is often . . . qualified. And of course it's an interesting comparison to consider the legacy, for example, of Arkady Danilov, who ran the Bolshoi Ballet for thirty years until the late 1980s, a period that was widely considered to be a golden age . . . and free from the sort of drama and scandal that . . ."

Marina moves quickly, regretting her decision to bring the outside world into our own. The voices are silenced. I hear the radiator reconsider whether it's really spring yet. She turns her back to me and pulls the blanket close. "Turn the light off, please. I'm tired."

I do. In the dark I feel her retreat from me.

"What happened to that splendid golden age, Ma?" I ask.

There's a long silence.

"They sold all the gold," she finally says.

THREE
DANSE SCANDAL

It takes a solid week for Daniela to regain conscious-
ness, and a week is a long time to endure suspicion. No
one has questioned me directly about that Friday night,
which I guess is a good sign. But all around me, in stereo
sound and sight, are the dropped voices and sidelong
glances. A few of my colleagues have walked up to me,
hands on hips, eyebrows arched with dutiful words of
congratulation: "Danse Sacrale?" they say with a hint in
the corner of their mouths. "I didn't know anyone was
performing that anymore."

As if the Bolshoi were charting unknown waters.

Aside from the pianist assigned to accompany me during my four minutes, not a single person at the theater
has spent more than forty seconds alone with me since
the accident. Arkhipova sent a note saying that it was up
to me to choose a trainer. I chose none. Nina, since the
day when she heard about my solo, has artfully avoided

me, visiting Daniela on her own. Stas, too, is keeping a low profile, staying in the theater shops. Working late.

So when I get the news that Daniela is awake, alert, and asking for me, I head straight to the hospital. Alone. A good idea, it turns out. Because for the first time (and at the worst possible time) Daniela is ready to put me center stage in her drama. I have hardly even sat down next to her bed when she throws her bomb in my lap.

"Lana, I know how you feel about the Bolshoi. I know how you feel about Vartukh. And now I know what you are capable of."

"What do you mean?"

"That you could do this. You've always been stronger . . ."

"Do what?" I begin.

Daniela rolls her eyes. I think that's what she is doing. She raises a plastered arm. "This!" she shouts in a whisper.

I shake my head slowly. Then faster.

"You're delirious. You aren't thinking clearly. I am not capable of this. Not in the least." I say this as I remember how I dug my nails into Stas's arm, hissing; *Don't. Do. It.*

Daniela is silent. And her silence is worse than her accusation.

"*Daniela, milaya,* believe me," I beg. "How many times have I said it? That I would walk away from the Bolshoi . . . for anything better. If you are not better than this half-savage ballet, for God's sake—what is?"

She turns away from me. I see her grip the thin sheet in a weak fist.

"Dana," I start again. "Believe me."

My heart is beating out of control. Daniela takes ages to turn her head and study me. Her eyes are hot, desperate, as she whispers so low that I can hardly hear: "*I want to.*" She closes them tight. A single tear spills down her cheek, and a nurse enters with Arkhipova and Vartukh at heel.

"Visiting hours are over," says the nurse.

"Bullshit," I snap.

But Anna Dmitrievna already has my arm and is leading me out the door. Then she looks up and down the hallway and says this: "You leave for New York in seventy-two hours. I can see when anxiety interferes with work and so, for the good of the tour, I am arranging a press conference. When it is over, you too should put an end to this episode. Whatever nerves or stress or maybe it's guilt that you are feeling . . . for the good of the company, get it under control. I will see you at the airport on Monday."

It is a short speech. But it leaves a bruise on my forearm.

HALF DAZED I EXIT the building and walk toward the river. Heavy weather hangs over the western bank and I feel a chill wrap around my ankles. I pull my jacket tighter and walk until I am at the gates of Novodevichy. Daniela doesn't believe me. *I want to*, I hear her whisper.

I walk past the bored young woman selling maps at the ancient entrance gate and enter the convent grounds.

It's been many years since I last visited. But I immediately feel the same paradox—sublime peace, and below, buried disquiet. Tranquil, lovely, spiritual: Novodevichy is all these things. But with every step I feel unease under my soles.

I cross the open compound, lingering just a moment before the entrance to the main church. It is a compact cluster of turrets, each topped in a deep blue dome, studded in golden stars. They remind me of mushrooms— another object of Russian reverence. There are many kinds of *grib* in our forests, but the churches are most like the honey mushrooms, the psychedelic stalks, the fairy fungi. And the domes, too; we call them onion domes and paint them azure, but don't they resemble the red kerchief of the *mukhomor*? Under their peak is the all-seeing eye of God, painted with reverent brushes.

The church door opens and releases an old *babushka* in a winter coat and a cloud of incense. She passes me, muttering about cheap candles and hooligans.

I cross the compound and pass through the high ivy-covered arch that leads to the cemetery. Here, the quiet is deeper. The breeze is higher, uninterested in us walkers on earth. I wander through the graves, browsing the names, the dates, the expository mixed with tribute that marks the final resting place of so much beauty and terror. The dead of Novodevichy were persecuted. They lived without freedom. Their graves count the attempts to make the most of hardship—to write through coded silence, to dance in the face of fear. I don't want to pass judgment on the artists and writers and intellectuals who fought valiantly against the Soviet system. But they lost. No one remembers them. Not anymore.

Except maybe my mother. My mother, who worships the dissident poets and soulful folksingers. And falls asleep with the light on.

I am not my mother.

I don't have idols. Not one.

The path I am following leads me to a lonesome spot, a crumbling corner empty of crosses and full of weeds. A few of the graves have old photographs glazed in ceramic cameos. My eyes are naturally drawn to those, but not with any real interest. It's so quiet I think I can hear my heartbeat. The walls, close on three sides, keep the sun out and it feels like twilight at midday. I do a slow tour of the rounded annex and am just about to rejoin the main path when I notice it—a small white gravestone with a simple inscription: *Svetlana Dukovskaya 1944–*

It's not just the name that has stopped me. There are plenty of Svetlana Dukovskayas to be found. At least I think so. I mean, I haven't in fact found them. I wonder, for a moment, how hard I've been looking. But it's the lack of a death date that surprises me. It's unusual in Russia and especially in here, this famous and exclusive cemetery. I stand before it, this place where Svetlana Dukovskaya, who shares my grandmother's name, isn't.

Everyone has family in Novodevichy, my mother had said. I leave quickly.

• • •

BACK OUTSIDE THE CONVENT walls Moscow is an onslaught and the rain is closer. I see a TV news truck outside the hospital and remember what Anna has said about the press conference. I follow a loose group of journalists through the entrance and into a gloomy enclosure near the cafeteria. There are several rows of chairs and a podium with the Bolshoi logo affixed crookedly to its front. It seems appropriate—the famous columned façade at a tilt, like a sinking ship. I stand at the back with the cameramen. One of them cracks a stupid joke: "What jumps higher than a man in tights? A man in tights with a BMW up his ass."

When Vartukh and Arkhipova enter, the cameramen go quiet.

Anna Dmitrievna thanks everyone for coming, assures them that the incident has shaken the Bolshoi community, informs them of Daniela's improvement and certain permanent injuries, warns them that no questions will be entertained. With that grim prologue, she introduces Pavel Vartukh, artistic director of the Bolshoi Ballet.

This is what he has to say:

"The Bolshoi Theatre is the pride of Russia. I am a Russian. Yes, a Russian of Armenian descent. I was born in Yerevan, but I was raised in the Bolshoi. That makes me a child of Russian ballet. I intend to make that ballet once again an object of adoration not just of Greater Russia, but of the world. The man who attacked myself and Ms. Mitrokhin and then fled the scene made a declaration. One that I have reported to the police investigators and which they have given me permission to make public. He said, *The Bolshoi for the Russians.*"

Vartukh pauses, allowing this revelation to write itself into the story. The journalists scribble and tap at their phones. Their cameras click.

"I'm not surprised that my attacker showed a level of cultural ignorance. Terrorists and fanatics always do. But the irony is that the Bolshoi is what he believes he wants. Of course the Bolshoi, Russian like me, is more than the pride of all of the Russian-speaking people, more than Greater Russia or the former Soviet Union, more than the Motherland. The Bolshoi *is* Russia, and precisely for that reason, of priceless value to the entire world. Thank you. No further questions."

And with that Pavel Vartukh turns a mystery into a hate crime and nationalist campaign. The press swallows it greedily and adds its own lurid twists. Only in Russia can ballet-mania, homophobia, and blatant racism happily cohabitate a headline:

BOLSHOI BLAMES "IGNORANT NATIONALISTS!"
HATE CRIME OF PASSION?
RUSSO-EXTREMIST BEHIND BALLET DRIVE-BY!
ETHNIC CLEANSING AT THE BOLSHOI THEATRE?

I think back on Anna's instructions. After the press conference, I should put all guilty feelings aside and concentrate on my upcoming debut. For the sake of the Bolshoi Ballet. Which has now been made the target of some rogue ethnic supremacists. I get it. This story line saves me an interrogation. I may be a loose cannon with a crew cut, but I'm not a right-wing skinhead. I am, as they say, free to go.

LUDMILA KIRILOVNA IGNORES ME in class. For whatever reason, ever since Anna assigned me to the solo, it's like I'm the ghost dancer. No one corrects me, no one observes me, no one seems to see me. Not even when I am rehearsing a completely renegade version of the company repertoire.

You'd think, for all my mouthing-off about how an artist needs space to create and license to experiment, for all my loony suggestions that we use pogo sticks to drill our *entrechats* and jump ropes to train *port de bras*, for all my eye rolling over the minutia that makes my trainers stop the music and demand that I do it, this time, correctly—that I would be pleased to be left alone with my number.

I am.

I am extraordinarily pleased. Not to mention inspired and liberated and kind of on fire with what happens when I close the door of the low-ceilinged studio and whirl into my own Danse Sacrale.

But today I'm worried. Because as Anna Dmitrievna so stridently reminded me, on Monday I fly to New York, but no one has reviewed my interpretation. And it's a pretty wide interpretation. In fact, I've jettisoned the original almost entirely. First—by refusing to take "primitive" literally: I dance on pointe, and so does my pagan. No one, ever since Vaslav Nijinsky hobbled his

virgin in knee-high moccasins, has danced the Danse
Sacrale on pointe. And second—well, second and third
and fourth and fifth . . . I've changed everything about
the damn dance. Everything but its arc. Its physical
nature. Its emergence, energy, and exhaustion. In that
order. Everything else is recast by me and my spotlight.

Two days ago, as I was etching certain passages firmly
in my muscles, the pianist stopped and said simply: "So
this is how it's going to go down in New York?"

"You tell me," I had answered. "Is this how it should
go down in New York?"

He shrugged and cracked his knuckles. He's just a
kid, my pianist. Probably drafted from the conservatory
and not even paid. "This is the one that started a riot
when they first performed it, yeah?" he had asked.

I thought so. His head is full of technique and a
swarm of factoids: The Rite of Spring—*brisk, steady,
percussive. Premiered by Ballet Russes in Paris in 1913.
Dissonant tones and discordant movement scandalize
ballet audience. Stampede ensues. Musicians drowned
out by catcalls. Conductor struggles to keep orchestra
together. Choreographer calls out steps from the wings
for dancers made deaf to the music.*

I just kept working on this transition I had come up
with—sweeping from a lunge into a hollowed body
crawl and back into a nearly fifty-degree backbend. The
pianist kept talking.

"So. It's like the dance has a tradition, right? Of
breaking tradition, right? Is that what you're up to?"

"Let's just start from the top," I had said.

But now there is no more need to rehearse. I have mastered my solo. The only thing to do now is perform it. And yet, no one is asking me to. They can't possibly mean to wait until the dress rehearsal on the stage at the Metropolitan Opera House in New York City. Can they?

And so after class I approach Ludmila Kirilovna.

I ask her if she has a minute to stay behind. To watch my Danse Sacrale, which I feel is in good shape but which, I know, could only benefit from her instruction. She doesn't look at me while I'm saying this. She is busy making herself busy. Wiping down the barre as if she's a custodian, straightening the sheet music on the stand by the piano, pulling up her stocking, pulling up her stocking again, pulling up that damn, stubborn, droopy stocking again.

"Ludmila Kirilovna?" I ask.

"Lana—you want to dance with the big girls, you should not be asking me for permission," she says.

This makes no sense to me at all.

"Permission?" I ask. "Ludmila Kirilovna, you are my coach. I am asking you, respectfully, for your assistance and support. I am a junior company member and have been given a very great honor. It is my responsibility to prepare to my best ability. And frankly, it is your responsibility, too."

At that she jerks her head. Her eyes look strange. Wary.

"I am not responsible for you any longer, Lana. I'm sure your performance will be up to Pavel's standards. Why else would he have selected you?"

With that, she hurries from the room, leaving me with an unanswerable question: *Why else would he have selected you?* Why, indeed.

I pace the room, playing back in my mind that day in Arkhipova's office. The more I think about it, the more certain I am that *she* had selected me. Had she even mentioned Pavel Vartukh? Yes. To say that she had talked him into the idea of putting Danse Sacrale on the program in New York. *After all,* she had said, *it's meant to be a maiden dancing for her elders, is it not?*

A flash of alarm, and then it is gone. I will dance for whomever I choose. I am the Chosen One.

I march to the studio door, stick my head into the hallway and find my callow conservatory student.

"Come on, then," I say. "Let's start this scandal from the top."

FOUR
DEPARTURE

My mother wakes me on the day of my departure with breakfast in bed.

"Sorry, love, no currant tea. But everything else you like."

She's right. Oatmeal loaded with honey and raisins, toast with jam, fresh wild strawberries. My mother rocked this one. I smile at the substitute green tea and kiss her cheek. Marina's wearing a silk kimono. Her long hair is tied in a loose knot at her neck. Such a picturesque style, I think, though it reminds me of her spirit: becoming, but bound; elegant, but on the verge of coming undone. I tell her she's beautiful, because she is. She smiles.

She sits herself cross-legged at the foot of my bed and watches me eat. The television is muttering from the living room but Marina prattles over it, acknowledging the flight, my bags, the tour. All of them, she is basically saying, become realities tonight. When she runs out of things to say, she pops a few strawberries in her mouth. She finds something to say about the strawberries. They'll be tastier in another month.

I've polished off the oatmeal and I'm full, but I know if I move the tray, breakfast is over. If breakfast is over, Marina goes her way and I go mine, and the last conversation we will have shared before the first separation we've ever known will have been about currant tea and how they've stopped selling it at the store near Tishinsky Market. So I nibble slowly at the toast and ask my mother about Lincoln Center in New York City and the Metropolitan Opera House.

"Ah, the Met. The most beautiful opera house in the world," she says.

This surprises me. My mother, for all her conflicted loyalty, rarely allows for the Bolshoi to be bested.

"Especially at night," she adds, pulling her feet closer under her robe. "Well, maybe mostly at night. In the daylight it is pleasing enough, the plaza. It has nice symmetry, a tasteful fountain. It sits up off the street, but still invites the city. I like that. But at night, Lanochka. Oh, it's just beautiful." She shakes her head, lost in the past I don't know. "The way those arches light up with gold. Like lanterns. Like Aladdin's cave, except you can see the treasure inside."

"And the stage?" I ask. "Bigger than ours?"

Marina's face drops. "Oh. I don't think so, no. But I never danced on it. So I don't know."

"Not ever?" I ask.

"Not ever, no. I left before I had the chance."

I wait a beat. This is where the story always ends. If I backpedal, we might cross over the gap.

"But you went to performances there, surely."

"One or two, yes," she says noncommittally. "I was just a student and I didn't have much money. I went when my teachers at Juilliard provided tickets. And . . ."

There's a long pause.

"And?"

"I went to concerts. I had more invitations to concerts, I guess, than to ballets."

"What sort of concerts?" I ask.

"Oh. Piano concertos. A symphony or two. That kind of thing."

She looks at me blankly. Then at my tray. "You're done?"

I nod. But she doesn't move.

"I could have stayed there, Lana," she says. "Imagine that. And then maybe—maybe—I would have danced on that stage. But then. Everything would be different."

"That's true," I say patiently. "There wouldn't be me, for example."

Now she moves to pick up the tray. But I stop her. "Or is that not what you meant?"

Marina shrugs. Her knot is looser. Her hair falls down the front of her kimono. "Yes," she says. "That. And of course I would not have danced with the Bolshoi. And I would never trade either of those things."

"But you did," I say. "You gave the Bolshoi up. And don't say it was for me."

"Of course it was, Lana. How can a single mother make any other choice?"

We've been here before.

My mother stands and goes to the window. She closes the *fortochka*, the small window in a window that provides the only ventilation in the old buildings that even after a half century have not learned how to transition gracefully through the seasons.

I don't want the *fortochka* closed. I want to smell the hint of warmth in the trees outside. I want to invite a breeze into the room, and I know my mother well enough to know she wants that, too. She doesn't even realize the symbolism of her actions. Closing that small window against the promise of something new.

"If you came back just to dance with the Bolshoi," I say patiently, "you certainly had another choice."

"What do you mean? Of course I came back to dance with the Bolshoi. And that's what I did. I danced with the Bolshoi and then I chose not to. I chose to be a mother who could care for her child. On her own. Without any interference."

It's a strange word: "interference." I shake my head at her archaic determination. Was it really so recent that a pregnant girl had to defend her abandonment by declaring any support from whoever knocked her up as "interference"?

"You mean without a husband," I say.

"Oh, Lana—that was not an option," she snaps as though I'm the one being old-fashioned.

She stoops to clear the breakfast away, but I'm not

done. I'm just getting started. I grab the half-eaten toast from the plate. Then I grab the plate. "Ma, I don't care about whoever he was. Spit on it. So I'm a bastard. Whatever. But don't lie to yourself. Because then you are lying to me."

She's looking at me now. Trapped. Closer to confession than I've ever seen her.

"If you came back to be the star of the Bolshoi, then you should have shone longer," I say, quieter now. "You were just a girl, Ma. Nobody plucks an American girl from New York who's never even danced on the stage and invites her to join the Bolshoi. I don't care how talented you were, your path was paved . . ."

I stop because I see what she is hearing.

"I don't mean that you did something . . . *ne tak*, something wrong. I don't mean that. I know you got there on merit, Mama. But how did you know that? How did you get here?" What I mean is: *What made a girl with no parents think she'd find a real home in a country that spit her out and then fell apart?*

I got two of Marina's three names. I should have a name from my father as well, but Lana Nobody-evna Dukovskaya has a rather bereft ring. So I got Viktor's— the grandfather I never knew. The one who was killed. *A terrible accident*, Marina always called it—Viktor Dukovsky's death just a few months after he brought his daughter to New York without her mother. I know even less about my grandmother. Just her name. I remember the first time I asked. *Kak zvali tvoyu mamu?* What did they call your mama? I remember how it was like playing a sharing game with a playmate: *My favorite color is pink; what's your favorite color? My mama is Marya; who's your mama?*

Sveta, she told me. Even then, at age five, I could put it together. "Sveta"—short for Svetlana. "Lana"—an American sort of Svetlana. So there I was: Lana Viktorovna Dukovskaya. My missing relatives branded right into my name. Along with the void of my father.

"Why did you come back to Russia when you did?" I ask her now.

"I couldn't come back sooner. I came back as soon as I could."

"But why?"

This is always the end. The dead end. *Why?* Because when I ask why, my mother doesn't hear one question. She hears a million questions. And she doesn't have all the answers. So I don't even get one.

I toss the stupid toast on the tray. I miss. Now there's jam on the floor. I reach down to clean it up and hear my mother say:

"I was looking for someone."

I right myself slowly, but the blood is still rushing the wrong way in my head.

"Who were you looking for?"

She rubs her eyes. She reknots her hair. She pulls the kimono closer.

"Doesn't matter. *Ne nashla.* I didn't find . . ."

In Russian she doesn't have to tell me whom she didn't find. *Ne nashla.*

"Why doesn't it matter?" I demand. I'm losing

patience. "I think it sure as shit matters, Marina. Because here I am. Here I am, so you must have found someone. And why you won't tell me who . . ."

Marina stands. She's out the door. Plates clatter in the kitchen. A teacup breaks. Breakfast is over.

STAS IS MY ANGEL again. Now that they've arrested some nationalist punk hooligan from Lyubertsy with a criminal record a mile long and charged him with "aggravated assault on an important cultural individual," Stas is back on his bike. He's happy to cross town to pick me up, and just as happy to sneak me onto one of the theater's main stages from the scene shop access. I have seven hours before I have to be at the airport; practicing my solo before an audience of zero seems like a good way to spend them.

But when we arrive I see Vartukh's car parked out front. I hadn't anticipated anyone else coming to the theater before departure, least of all him. It's Monday, the theater's Sabbath. There should be nothing happening but my Danse Sacrale.

Stas parks on the curb of a side street. I follow him through a gate into the shop. Inside we're greeted by a radio left on overnight. Terrible pop music made worse by being just slightly off its frequency. Static mixed with an auto-tuned whine about "last night, our first night, a dark night, a lost night." Stas snaps the radio off and stretches.

"So, the concert stage?" he asks.

"Yeah. I guess."

He pulls keys from a drawer in his worktable and I follow him through a corridor littered with papier mâché and canvas and klieg lights. My mind is back home, with my mother and the sadness of her voice: *I was looking for someone.* We are nearly at the stage door when I hear the music coming from the other side. Stas pulls the door open and it greets us: Stravinsky's *The Rite of Spring.* I catch my breath and push past him. Nina is on the stage.

"My dear, your footwork is perfect. Really. I quite like the extra beat you give the *frappé* jumps. But remember your audience, please. They are not watching your feet, after all. They are watching your fate. Can we try it again from the top and, this time, with some urgency?"

Pavel Vartukh's thick mane of hair is just visible in the stage lights. He is stretched languidly in the first row, one arm propped on the chair back, the other nestled across his chest in a sling.

I watch Nina dance the beginning of the solo. My solo. I can hear nothing but her feet—the speedy pawing of her studied technique. The knocking clatter of her eagerness to please. A minute and a half in and I see her forget the dance entirely, even if she hasn't forgotten the steps. I see her trying to catch the music and failing. I see my friend Nina as a subtle hostage of someone else's timing. I'm about to move farther into the darkened auditorium but Stas holds me back. I turn and look at him. His finger is on his lips. He retreats. I follow him back into the corridor.

"What's that all about?" I begin. My voice is too tight.

"I don't know, Lana."

I start to pull away from him, ready to make a scene, but he stops me.

"You want to go to New York, right?"

I don't have to nod.

"So go. Forget you saw this. Your flight is this evening. If you confront them, you disrupt everything."

I hesitate.

In our silence I hear Vartukh's voice again: "We can work on it in New York, Nina. It's not ready yet."

Stas is still holding my arm, guiding me back down the corridor. Now I'm cursing, but just out of habit. Whatever it is I am angry about, it's not really about Vartukh or Nina or the imperfect performance I've just witnessed. It's not about the games someone is playing with this whole "addition to the program," or the growing certainty I feel that Nina and I are being squared off for battle. So what's it about?

Back in the scene shop, I grab a bottle of rubber cement from Stas's worktable and hurl it against the cinder-block wall. Its shatter leaves a slug. We watch it slide behind a shelf of paint canisters.

"Feel better?" asks Stas.

"Nope."

Stas turns and starts fiddling with a glue gun lying handily nearby. I'm watching him, my mind blank, until this crazy image of me on a rampage with a glue gun jolts me out of it. I grab my dance bag and pull out my shoes. Stas puts down the gun and raises an eyebrow.

"What?" I ask.

He shrugs.

"Stage is free, isn't it?"

"Maybe I should check for you."

I sigh and watch him disappear once more into the corridor. A minute later he is back—the coast is clear. "Forget what you saw," he says. "And dance. Go on. I have work to do."

The stage is dark. I snap on auxiliary lights, dim reminders of how alone I am. The disc is still in the portable player at the front of the stage and I cue the music to listen through as I lace my shoes on. From where I am sitting on the edge of the stage I can see the faint imprints of Nina's attempt. She was wearing soft shoes—her *Rite of Spring* follows tradition. It is a ballet of natives, pagans garbed in shapeless sheaths and felt boots. For a minute, I regret my decision to break with tradition, to forgo primitivism and dance on pointe. I try to talk myself back up. It was a smart move—adapting the choreography to keep on my toes. But this makes me laugh out loud. I've been a fool. No coach, no review, no presentation. Did I really think they were just going to let me loose on New York's Metropolitan Opera stage to reinterpret an iconic dance without any oversight from the directors? How utterly arrogant I've been. Now I know. I am not to be let loose at all. I am a decoy. But why?

The music ends. I start it over, working my body through isolations: neck, shoulders, ribs, abdomen, hips. All of them isolated. Like me. I'm ready to perform. If this is to be my only chance to dance my "Danse Sacrale," so be it. It will have to be my best.

I dance it through once. Then again. I rework the end, the collapse, adding several beats to my final reach for the sky, letting my body hang from my own desperate fingertips, feeling the weight of all my ignorance fall away from my frame and landing on the floor like a mattress that will brace my fall. I feel that suspension in my body and could swear the music follows my lead.

I'm winded. I've never danced these four minutes so fully—and the effort has nursed a small lingering seed of euphoria. I run my hand through my cropped hair and feel electricity. I lean to the floor and grip my ankles, which are ready to take flight. I rub one calf muscle and then the other. They sing, hitting high notes. I feel a hot flame in my belly. I think it's conviction. What I have done to the Sacrale is too good to be a decoy. It is too promising to be a premise. It is worth more than whatever Vartukh and Arkhipova think they will get out of it.

I pound my forehead in frustration. I need to make sure that they see me. I shouldn't have kept it to myself. What if I am too late?

There's a sound from the back of the theater. I shade my eyes against the lights and watch a figure emerge from the dark. My mother is walking down the aisle, her head bowed low, her pace slow.

"Ma?" I ask. "What are you doing here?"

"I wanted to see it," she says. "You never offered to show me. But I wanted to see your solo."

Her head is still bent. The part in her hair seems to me as livid as a new scar. I'm about to answer defensively, to explain that this is the first time it has been ready to see, when she lifts her face. Her eyes are full of tears. She is smiling.

"It is absolutely marvelous. I've never seen anything so exciting, Lana."

"Really?"

"Really."

"They won't let me dance it," I say.

"Have they even seen it?"

I shake my head. "They don't need to. I don't think they ever intended for it to be mine. Nina will dance it. If anyone does."

"She will never dance it like that," she says.

I smile. Obviously.

"Do you know it? I mean the original choreography."

She shrugs. "What's to know? Hop, hop, hop—muscle spasm, arm flail . . . But I love what you have done with it. Really. I think it's exquisite."

This makes me laugh. Marina is not a fan of avant-garde. Even when it's a hundred years old.

We stand in silence. The auditorium is vast—an enormous warehouse of ambition, anticipation, triumph and disappointment. But at this moment there are no hard feelings to be found in its walls.

"Come dance with me, Ma."

I turn my back so I can't see her if she declines. I step to the disc player and cue the music once more. My heart skips a beat when I hear her jump lightly to the stage. She is tying up her long skirt, slipping off her sandals. The music begins and my mother is transformed into a spirit. A spirit hounded by bodies. A soul hunted by ghosts. She is light on her bare feet and heavy in her hands. She embodies the sacrifice implied in the music without even trying. I am dancing near her, but not yet with her, and I can't help but admire the way she moves even as I hate its implicit tragedy.

We are halfway through the piece, my mother improvising the ruts and stammers of an ill-fated maiden, when I feel her hand on mine. In an instant the dance has changed. Marina, still limp and pliant as a puppet, is now pulling the strings. I feel her direction, feel her repel me and encourage me. She is muting my outrage, cooling my heat, lowering me to earth. She is offering me an alternative. Maybe it is a disguise. Maybe it is a mask. Certainly it is easier to wear than a crown of a martyred maiden.

When the music ends, it takes me a moment to understand: Marina is the only coach I have. And she has just made my dance sacred by sharing it.

"You have more talent than I ever had," she says as she secures her hair in a knot. "You can make your stage anywhere. If it's not this one, let it be the one in that Aladdin's cave in New York. And if it's not that one, let it be the boardwalk on Brighton Beach. It doesn't matter where you find your spotlight, Lana. Only that you never abuse it. And that you never regret it."

This advice, neither predictable nor obvious, etches itself in my mind. Her physical submission has already planted itself in my body. I take five steps and hug my mother fiercely.

Two hours later she puts me and my suitcase in a taxi and a letter in my hand. She taps on the glass and I roll the window down. "Shine bright," she says. Then she turns and walks away.

ACT TWO
THINGS SACRED
MANHATTAN

FIVE
BRAIN FREEZE

AFTER EIGHT HOURS IN the air, I have a mean cramp. It's not in my calves, though they have been flexed up against the back of seat 33D since Greenland. That's when I turned on a romantic comedy starring a blonde professional and a hapless artist with two Saint Bernards. I watched the whole damn thing through the heart-shaped gap of my knees. The physical demands of a transatlantic flight in Aeroflot's coach class are nothing a dancer can't survive. It's the knot in my head that won't go away.

Marina's letter was one page long. It was loaded. And empty. For eight hours its message gripped my brain like a vise.

Darling Lana,

When I was a girl I had dreams. Not the kind of dreams that you wish will come true. The kind of dreams that do come true. The dreams told me

I would be alone. Until I had you. When I had you, the dreams stopped.

But I had a dream last night. I had a vision of you onstage at Lincoln Center. You stepped through the curtains and brandished your fists. It frightened me. I felt certain you were raising your hands to defend yourself. I hurried to the theater to tell you. To stop you from going and to keep you safe. But when I saw you dance, Lana, I knew that my vision was of your hands raised in triumph. I knew that you are destined to be the star I never was. I would never forgive myself if I kept that from happening. So I said nothing. Instead, I danced with you, selfishly allowing myself a taste of your victory, your beautiful gift.

Now I am home and I am frightened again. Because I stopped trusting my visions long ago. Once I had a dream that I would see my mother again. I never did. I have not told you very much about her, Svetlana Dukovskaya. All I can tell you is that she never returned to me. So I don't trust my dreams. Please be careful, Lana, and please return to me.

I love you with all my beating heart,

Mama

She had written: *with all my beating heart.*
I read: *with all my broken heart.*

OUR BUS FROM THE airport slows to a crawl and then stops altogether, trapping me in a blinding glare of sunset. Nina is sitting behind me and she wriggles fingers over my seat. "Manhattan, Lana! Look! There's the Empire State Building."

I shield my eyes to look out the window. We are like a whale in a school of pilot fish. All I can see are the tops of the cars below; the occasional thigh in the passenger seat; the lone arm of a commuter, his white shirt rolled up to his elbow, dangling a smoking cigarette into the toll plaza. I lean forward a bit more, and as I do the quick sinking sun shoots an orange flare across the river. In its wake I see the whole legendary skyline.

New York City in the last of the daylight is blue-green and placid, like the weathered underwater castle of a fish tank. But it's a castle of turrets and spires and towers ten miles long, and it's growing across the horizon like urban coral.

Someone in a car below us lays on his horn. I plug earbuds into my phone and sink into English lyrics I don't fully understand, but believe to be about me. As long as the music is playing I can't use the phone to call Marina and promise to return. As long as the music is playing I'm neither home nor away.

BY THE TIME WE arrive at our hotel, it's deep dusk, and now my body does feel cramped. Anna Dmitrievna gathers us in the lobby. She's full of instructions and warnings and "tips." She knows her way around this city, Anna does, and she waves her hand breezily this way and that. "Ruby Foo's," she says. "Ollies, Serafina, there's a deli on Seventy-third Street. Gray's Papaya if you're willing to risk a performance for an excellent hot dog. Of course you needn't eat a big meal in any case. It's two A.M. in Moscow, so I recommend Jamba Juice, maybe a small snack from the coffee shop in the lobby, and you should all be early to bed. We have rehearsal tomorrow at ten."

On the third floor, the girls from the corps pile out of the elevator. The principals and primas have their single accommodations one floor up, but we are packed three and four to a double room. Nina and I will be week-long roommates with Olga, a taciturn dancer going on her second decade in the corps; and Tatiana, whom I last saw sucking up to a bastard with a pool cue.

I linger in the hallway as Tatiana struggles with the electric card key. Olga is already positioned behind her, ready to grab the best side of the best bed, which-ever one that might be. Nina is prancing up and down the hallway like she's about to enter stage right. Or maybe she just has to pee. I ask. She giggles. "Aren't you just so stiff from that nightmare plane? My God, I think I'll never get my head back on my neck prop-erly."

I don't answer. But my hand drifts to the letter in my jacket pocket.

Tatiana finally succeeds in getting the door open, and in minutes our hotel room is transformed into her per-sonal boudoir. She's already filling the tub. Nina is at the window, opening the curtains with a flourish. Our view is of a narrow airshaft. Across it, a tiny woman in too-large sweatpants is vacuuming the floor of an empty office. I can see a row of identical cubicles. Except for one that is lined with bobblehead desktop toys. The office jokester.

"Let's get out of here, Nina," I say.

WE HEAD SOUTH ON Broadway toward Lincoln Center, just five blocks away. At 64th street, we dart across a busy traffic axis and stand before the wide plaza set up off the street. Directly ahead of us is the Metropolitan Opera House, the Met, its five portals illuminated and spectacular. It is flanked on either side by its acolytes—two more theaters, separate and not equal. They, too, are spilling golden pools of light from their glassy symmetrical façades.

Nina takes my hand and pulls me up the wide stairs leading to the fountain in the center of the plaza. It explodes into its own symphony and the sound of the street drops away. We've arrived.

It's ten minutes till seven: showtime. Simultaneous curtain calls are drawing the public into the warmth of the foyers surrounding us. We watch their tiered progress through the windows and up escalators and grand staircases until they disappear into the unseen spectacle of their evenings.

Nina and I are left in the plaza, two of a handful of unticketed silhouettes swimming in the pool of Lincoln Center's night-lights. Nina bounces on the balls of her feet, delighted as a child. I give her a little push, launching her into a circuit of manic *piqué* turns around the fountain. "I feel like the silly pink ballerina that springs up in the center of a jewelry box!"

I follow her figure darting between the watery curtains
of the fountain, wishing I could snatch some of her exu-
berance. I raise my eyes again to the entrance, adorned
with banners announcing upcoming performances. One
of them is ours. They've used an old stock image. The
graceful shoulder under the gauzy scarf could be any
dancer: a member of the corps or a celebrated soloist or
even just a stand-in model with nice skin.

Marina's praise whispers in the high spring night. I
close my eyes against the splendor of this place, New
York's cultural cathedral. I imagine my mother standing
before it like Aladdin, rubbing a hopeful brass lamp.
But I feel empty. She has doused my joy with her pain.
I imagine my anger as the genie bottled up inside—stiff,
sullen and unwilling to come out. In spite of the warm
breeze. In spite of the golden light. In spite of spring. In
spite of New York.

In spite.

WE TAKE ANNA'S ADVICE and stop at Jamba Juice on
the way back to the hotel. The girl behind the counter
repeats our order and then asks us a half dozen ways
if we want something different. Bigger maybe? Better
maybe? A free shot of this? A boost of that? Smoothied?
Soy-ed? With a side of? We shake our heads no. She
takes our money and hands us two enormous drinks.
We can't immediately decide which is my "razzaman-
tioxidant," and which is Nina's "strawberry surf," so
we walk back up Broadway trading back and forth.

All this time I've not said a word to Nina about what

I saw on the stage before we left Moscow. But now that the only things between us and rehearsal tomorrow are two brain-freeze-inducing smoothies, it's time.

"What are they telling you about Danse Sacrale?" I ask.

Nina coughs and pounds her sternum with a dainty fist. "Oy, that's cold," she says in a strangled voice.

My teeth chatter. A frozen raspberry seed becomes my nemesis.

"They tell me that I suck," she finally says with a sidelong glance.

"When did they ask you to start rehearsing it?"

"The same day they asked you," she says. "Lana, I'm sorry. I didn't know how to tell you. I mean, at first I assumed that they would explain it themselves. I thought they would tell us—who was doing what day or who was understudy or whatever. And then Anna Dmitrievna said I really shouldn't mention it. So I didn't know what to think. I didn't want to say something that would make you, you know, blow up. I didn't want to be the one who caused you to get booted from the tour. Or even . . ."

Nina blocks the next thought with a long draw on her straw and another fraught cough.

"Or even from the company?" I finish for her. "Do you think I'm that close to being thrown out, Neen? Do you think my fuse is so short? That I would make such a scene they would ax me?"

Nina shrugs. I can see that's exactly what she thinks. We're still walking. I'm afraid if we stop, so will the honesty.

"Talk to me, Nina. What do you know?"

"Nothing. I swear. I don't know anything. Only that they told me I should prepare the solo. I asked if they meant as a sub or maybe for one performance, but they just said that the program wouldn't be fixed until we arrive in New York. And no, I don't think they're going to throw you out. Why would they bring you on tour if they were?"

Even as she says it, I feel her thoughts run right into mine. *Why else would Pavel have chosen you?* Ludmila Kirilovna had asked, too. Why would they bring me on tour without a role, without a reason, without even much evidence that they want me to succeed? What would prove an easier way to get rid of me than leaving me at home, nursing a grievance? A disastrous debut maybe? A temper tantrum abroad?

"Vartukh said that they were sending you as a gesture," Nina says softly.

This stops me dead. "A *what*?"

"Those very words. 'A gesture toward Marina Viktorovna.'"

The light at the corner turns green. A wave of headlights pass over us as we wait to cross Broadway. I think I see distrust illuminated on Nina's face. I'm pretty sure she never believed that I had anything to do with the attack, but maybe she's a better actress than I give her credit for. I can't even say for certain that Daniela believes me, and Nina is even more impressionable. So now she has yet another reason to suspect me. She thinks my mother has pulled influence. She has no idea how wrong that is.

"She didn't even want me to come," I say now. But I'm thinking of the letter in my pocket and its confession: *I would never forgive myself.* I'm thinking of Marina's parting words: *Shine bright.*

"Vartukh says you have a patron."

Marina Dukovskaya is no patron. She's a phantom.

"That's crap," I say less poetically.

We're back on the block of our hotel. The sidewalk is empty, but I'm afraid of the lobby. I grab Nina by the elbow. She looks at me with guileless blue eyes.

"Whatever happens tomorrow, will you promise me that you'll tell me everything you know?" I plead. "No matter how bad it looks for me? No matter what they say about my mother? Just promise me you won't keep me in the dark. Please?"

She nods. Once meekly. Once more forcefully.

I let go of her. We don't move. "Which version is it?" I ask.

Nina looks at me, a question.

"Which version of Danse Sacrale were you rehearsing with Vartukh?"

"He called it the 'Svetlana Variation.'"

SIX
SCREAM BECOMES A YAWN

I'm woken by the two-tone chirp of an incoming text message. I reach across Nina, curled up like a kitten under the scratchy coverlet, and knock half a dozen things off the bedside table before I find my phone.

There are four messages. They are all from my mother. Call me, they all say. So I do. But all I get is the unhelpful response that Marina's phone is *vremenno nidostupen*. Temporarily unavailable.

I start to write a text response: I'll call later. Evening Moscow time. But by now my anger is awake, too. I feel the punch of doubt: *as a gesture to Marina Viktorovna*. I wonder again at the veiled hints from Arkhipova about my mother speaking on my behalf. About my mother's likely disappointment if I didn't take her offer. At the time I had thought how little she knew my mother. Then the paradox: distance and time don't always add up. Anna Arkhipova, as removed as she is, has known my mother for longer than I have. Such a strange thought.

I hear the sounds of Olga in the bathroom, of Tatiana's iPod leaking bad pop music into the morning. I'm in a too-small hotel room with three witnesses, one of whom knows I'm somebody's "gesture." I delete the reply without sending it, turn my back to the room and plug into the song that is fast becoming my touchstone. The song that implies that it's perfectly normal to have dreams of the dead, dreams of the unknown, dreams so real. *Dreams I no longer trust,* is what Marina wrote.

A few minutes later, Olga emerges from the bathroom in a cloud of steam.

"Good morning," she mutters as I rise to take my turn. "My shampoo is the one with panthenol-D and essence of cacao. It's very expensive. But you can use it, since you hardly have any hair."

Believe it or not, that's Olga being kind. I thank her.

When I step out of the shower Nina is at the mirror, brushing her teeth. She shoots me a frothy smile and spits into the sink.

"You kick," she says.

"You snore," I say.

"You lie." She drops her robe and steps into the shower with a squeal. New York City's hotels don't joke with the hot water.

DOWNSTAIRS THE SMALL COFFEE shop is crowded with Bolshoi. Anna Dmitrievna is nowhere to be seen, but Vartukh is sitting at a small table alone. I grab a yogurt from the buffet and approach him.

"Good morning."

"Have a seat, Lana," he says. He looks tired.

I sit and open the yogurt, waiting for him to speak. I stir, waiting. Then I eat. Finally, when I'm done I say, "Pavel Artemovich, is there anything I should know about the program? Perhaps there is something you want to tell me about the variation?"

He looks at me, but I don't think he sees me. I don't think he sees anything. For a minute I wonder if it's true, the gossip about how hard he's taken Daniela's injuries. He seems so absent, uncertain, not his usual cocksure self. He seems lost. Is he lost without *her*?

"The solo?" I clarify.

He shifts in his seat. He tries to slurp the last of his coffee, but his cup is already empty. "Naturally, yes." He nods. "The solo."

"Is it still mine, Pavel Artemovich?" I ask quietly. "The Danse Sacrale?"

Finally, his eyes focus on me. They are not lascivious. They are not calculating. They are not offering me anything, and I'm almost ashamed I have asked. I think of Daniela and the tears on her terrible face when she told me she wanted to believe me.

Pavel speaks for only the third time since I've joined him. "Why else would you be here, Lana?"

Then he rises and leaves the room.

• • •

THERE IS STILL NO answer to that question. The question that dogged me all that morning and the next. Nor is there an answer from my mother, who doesn't pick up the phone. Marina has gone quiet. I don't know what sort of gesture that might be.

Now it's thirty-odd hours until opening night and still there is no final program. I've watched two run-throughs of *Les Sylphides*; witnessed the drama that unfolded when Larisa demanded a new partner; and been called on once to fill in for Nadia, who said she couldn't dance on account of cramps. I know every beat of the *Corsaire* suite and every step of the waltz from *The Sleeping Beauty*. But I still don't know if I, or anyone, will perform the Danse Sacrale.

Soon, too, I will know every inch of the corridors of the fourth floor of the Juilliard School, where we've been given two rehearsal studios. When Vartukh calls for another run-through of the first act of *The Sleeping Beauty*, I slip out the door and away from the endless strains of Tchaikovsky.

I head straight for the far end of the hallway, where a small photo gallery hangs on a deserted stretch of corridor. I approach it again: a thirty-year-old picture of some famous instructor as she corrects the line of extension *à la seconde*. The instructor, dramatic and wreathed in beaded necklaces, is looking directly into the camera. Her pupil shows only her back. Her raised arm and long neck frame her teacher's stern face. The caption reads, GRETA VON SCHLIEF, JUILLIARD BALLET MASTER 1975–1999.

It doesn't identify the student. But I think I recognize the faceless dancer. I recognize the effortlessness of her leg as it floats just beyond Greta von Schlief's fingertips. I recognize the smooth arc of her elbow. I recognize the loose strand of hair fishing in the wave of her spine.

It came as a shock yesterday when I discovered the photo, and I hurried away from it as if I were late for the rehearsal that I have no part in. But since then, I've returned to the wall once, twice. And each time I am more certain: the young dancer is Marina, a student at the Juilliard School, a girl marking time between two lives I never knew. The certainty is comforting. At least this much of her story has proof.

I glance out the window, out onto the fountain in the Lincoln Center plaza. I place my hands on the high windowsill and lift first my leg and then my arm, mirroring the pose in the picture. I raise my chin to pull my whole body higher in a salute. A salute to my mother, who has stopped sending me text messages.

As if in response, the fountain shuts off. I watch the liquid trajectory of the last jet collapse silently into the pool.

I drop my pose and return to rehearsal.

THE COMPANY HAS FINISHED a last-minute blocking change in the final act of *The Sleeping Beauty* and is milling about, waiting instructions. Vartukh looks at the clock. "We have fifteen minutes till break," he says, rubbing the back of his neck absently. "Nina, let's see your Sacrale."

It's an interesting phenomenon, the live wire that runs through a dance company and tethers it with a collective charge. Twenty dancers hear Vartukh's words; twenty dancers strike a different pose of disinterest. They adjust their hair, slide into stretches, retie their shoes, check their phones, or gaze at the floor, hands on hips. Twenty dancers turn their blank faces away from me. But all twenty are vibrating with the same energy that has made me break out in a sweat.

Nina throws me a quick glance as she removes her pointe shoes and pulls on the soft slippers of the traditional Chosen One. The sound guy cues the music, filling the room with bombastic brass and pounding kettledrums. Nina stands in the center, untouched by the ominous rhythms. I watch, fascinated by how deaf her sacrificial maid is to the sounds of her doom. I know this is not the choreography. This is Nina's real brain freeze. I hold my breath, caught between hope and despair for my friend . . . my competition.

Then she begins to move. Her feet shuffle, her shoulders slump. She jerks her head against the flute's sharp whip, just as Chosen Ones from time immemorial have. Of course, by "time immemorial," I mean only the last century. But that's the key. Because though it's only a hundred years old, Stravinsky's *Rite* is supposed to transport us to a pagan pre-civilization. To a time when Spring was cruel. We're supposed to believe, watching the Chosen One dance for her life, that within her destruction lies all of creation. And we're supposed to be complicit in her fate. We are more than witnesses. We are participants.

But there is none of that here on the fourth floor of Juilliard. The menacing melody crawls across the floor, but I feel the dancers on the sidelines step away from its slither. They are watching, yes. Watching as Nina circles the floor in proscribed fits and starts. She has not fumbled the steps, for the steps themselves are fumbling. The problem is that Nina is already lifeless. I close my eyes and feel my own Danse Sacrale strain against my stillness. Is this my punishment for holding so many grudges? Against Marina? Against the Bolshoi? Against the promises of Spring?

Finally, the music ends and Nina bends double, panting and relieved.

There is a murmur in the room, but no applause. You never clap in rehearsal unless a fellow dancer has fallen or injured herself. Applause from your colleagues is a sure sign that you have messed up badly. Nina has not. She has done nothing to warrant special attention.

Vartukh says as much.

"Oy, Nina. Is that a joke? That's your idea of martyrdom? Monotony?"

Nina jerks upright. Her face is mottled with distress. The murmur in the studio dies. I'm a beat behind, the lyrics from a song haunting me. It's the song that I've been listening to since I boarded a plane for New York. A song that has become a compulsion, a soundtrack, a theme. A song about dreams so real, about silent fear: *scream becomes a yawn, shut up and carry on.*

Vartukh's face is also distressed, his tone venomous. "It's just not up to Bolshoi standards. And I really don't

know how I can help you with it. This is, technically, one
of the easiest of the interpretations, but you are clearly
unable to embody the tensions it demands."

He is still rubbing his neck as Nina babbles her apologies. I realize I am holding my breath. There is only one
way this can end. They have to ask me.

"Pavel Artemovich," I say as I step forward across the
invisible line that every dancer sees. The one that marks
the sidelines. They are both looking at me and I see relief
on their faces. Nina knows that by taking the solo, I will
save her, not sink her. Pavel, too, appears grateful. He
nods at the sound engineer to cue the music.

I take my starting position. But when the raucous first
bars of music end, the dramatic pause is interrupted by
the slam of the studio door. Anna Arkhipova is clatter-
ing across the studio, stealing my stage.

The sound engineer kills the music.

"What is going on here?" she asks the room. Her
voice is acid. There is silence in response. The answer,
after all, is obvious. What is going on is a rehearsal.

"You are completely off schedule," she splutters, thrown
by her own outburst. "Forty minutes over lunch break."

Shuffling from the sidelines. A sigh from Vartukh.
And then he shrugs and holds his right hand high in an
old-fashioned gesture of magnanimity. As if he is a vis-
count and Anna a rich grand dame who has demanded
the mazurka over a minuet.

"All of you: break," he commands the troupe, his
eyes not leaving Anna's. "We resume in an hour."

Nina hurries to join the others as they file out of the

studio. Vartukh turns his back on me. Anna crosses her arms and dares me with one single eyebrow to try to understand. I rise to her challenge. I stand my ground. I will not be dismissed.

"I don't need a break, Anna Dmitrievna. I haven't danced in two days."

Vartukh is crossing to the corner where he left his cashmere sweater and smooth leather man-purse.

"Could you stay, please, Pavel?" I ask. "I would like to show you my variation. You see, I've worked very hard on it, and whatever you are—"

"Are you trying to sabotage the Danse Sacrale, Lana?" Anna interrupts.

"Of course not. I'm trying to dance it."

"Was Nina's performance unsatisfactory, Pavel Arte-movich?" she asks. She has used his two names like a double-barreled rifle.

He turns and his face is a mask. An ill-fitting one.

"Not at all. You can include it in Friday's matinee."

"Excellent."

Stravinsky is silent. *The Rite of Spring* has emptied itself from my body. In its place are the lyrics again: *shut up and carry on . . . the scream becomes a yawn.*

I can't. If I am to carry on, I can't shut up.

"Could you please tell me why I am here?" I demand. "I would like to know why you promised me a solo if you had no intention of letting me dance it."

Anna's face twists in contempt. "Has your mother taught you to extract promises from the Bolshoi, Lana?"

I flush red at the taunt. "At the very least, you could let me perform it for you. You could give it four minutes of your time. By all means, let Nina have the performance, but couldn't you at least show me the consideration of seeing what I have done with it?"

Anna opens her mouth to respond, but she is cut off.

"We've seen it, Lana," says Vartukh. "We've already seen your Danse Sacrale."

It's the most mysterious response I could have asked for.

They leave me alone in the studio. Alone with the music in my head: *thought I made a stand. Only made a scene.*

I WASTE NO TIME changing and bolting from the building. Outside, New York is innocent and oblivious. I consider calling Marina. I consider calling Stas. I consider the reckless and the rational and feel uninspired by both. I walk toward this big famous avenue called Broadway, feeling small and anonymous. My mind is blank. The only thing I know for certain is that I'm hungry. There's a food cart on the corner selling something that smells like sustenance. I join the line.

I'm digging in my bag for money when a voice asks: "Didn't anybody tell you not to eat meat on the street?"

He's addressing me in Russian.

Not the guy grilling chicken in the cart. Another guy. He's got sharp eyes and a soldier's haircut, and he's perched at the curb on a fantastic bike. I mean *fantastic*. A hound-of-hell kind of bike. Gleaming black body with mufflers like bazookas. Big buggy mirrors and headlights like a creature jumped from a Japanese anime. Its long leather seat begs for a passenger on back. He knows it. He grins and the gap in his front teeth draws a bit of my attention away from the motorcycle.

"It's just a Suzuki DR650," he says. His accent is peculiar, Americanized. "Never seen a girl drool over a dirt bike before."

I smile back. "I like it. It's a nice bike."

"Take a ride with me then," he says. His hands are in the pockets of a cracked leather jacket, casual.

I roll my eyes in response and step up to order. I point so as not to mispronounce something in front of this smug Russian-American in dark blue jeans who is watching me too closely.

"Seriously. I'm here to give you a ride." He's climbed off the bike and is pulling an extra helmet out of the seat compartment. "I have an invitation for you. To dinner. With an old admirer."

"You're not so old," I say. He's full grown, I can see that. But he's still growing into his mystery motorcycle man. It's a persona he's perfecting, and maybe it will become his signature role, but I don't have time to help him practice. "Thanks for the admiration, though."

"Oh no," he corrects me. "Not me. I'm just the messenger. Well, and the wheels, too."

He's at my side now and I'm struck by his size. The dude is big. But, like, proportionally. I'm used to tall, lithe men with compact muscles like studded gems. This guy is big because his hands are big. Because his smile is big. Because he is standing next to me now with a helmet in each hand and he smells of motorcycle grease and cologne.

"Seriously," he says. "I'd like to take you to meet someone. He's a fan of the Bolshoi, and he has been following your career."

"I don't have a career," I say. "Stick around and the stars will be out shortly."

"You are Lana Dukovskaya, no?"

The man selling chicken and rice from the cart wants to know if I want white sauce or red sauce. I can't answer because Mr. Motorcycle knows my name. I stumble for words. He answers for me: "It doesn't much matter— red or white. We're gonna toss that mess in the trash and feed you properly."

He's hit a wrong note.

"Listen," I snap. "I don't know how long it takes for a Russian boy to grow American balls, but I really don't want to see yours. I mean, it's cute that you know who I am. But you should know that the 'I'm your greatest fan,' line won't get me on the back of your bike. Not in Russia. And certainly not here. So don't get cozy just because you speak my language."

"And by 'your language' you don't mean dirt bike," he says. He's stepped back. I see he's recalculating. He has been too forward. He rubs his chin. I eye the trim goatee and the care that went into its grooming. I've underestimated him. He doesn't need to flirt. He's got more confidence than he needs. He's hiding it. This biker guy is an aesthete under his battered jacket. He may be just a year or so older than I am, but he's got decades of determination on me.

"You're right," he says. "Forgive me. Let's start again." He stands up straighter. "My name is Roma. I work for a man who would like to take you to dinner. His name is Georgi Levshik. He's waiting across town for us as we speak. Now—if you are busy or if you have your heart set on eating some third-world mess out of Styrofoam—I'll let Mr. Levshik know that he will have to make other plans. A 'rain check' as we call it here. But I imagine your nights will be quite busy after today. Your premiere, I believe, is tomorrow?"

"That's right."

The cart man hands me a plastic bag. I open it. Inside is, indeed, a Styrofoam container. I look up at this Roma, who smiles again—and again I fixate on those imperfect front teeth. Even the bike seems to be winking.

"And if I refuse dinner tonight, and decline your 'rain check,' too?" I ask. "What will this employer of yours do?"

He affects a look of concern. Again, the thoughtful chin rub. And then I see the playfulness leave.

"That's not actually an option, Lana."

He's dead serious.

I open the container. I look at Roma. I chuck the whole bag in the trash and hold out my hand for the helmet.

SEVEN
DINNER WITH GEORGI

Stas has a theory about girls who like bikes. He thinks we like a man at the wheel. But only if he's merely operating the controls. Not actually in control. "You don't drive a motorcycle," Stas likes to say. "It drives you." In other words, riding on the back of a motor-cycle is like diluting gender roles. It's like playing house but insisting that the house exists in zero gravity. That way, nobody has the upper hand.

But I know, as we drop down into the brick-walled roadway that bisects Central Park, that Suzuki Roma has the upper hand.

There are a million ways to correct this imbalance, I think. I don't know where we are going, but in the time it takes to get there I need to come up with an explanation as to why I allowed him to shanghai me. For me, if not for him. I'm trying them all out in my head as we exit the park and slink through the traffic. There's nonchalance: *I needed to get cross town, anyway*; humor: *I hope you charge less than the horse-and-carriage racket;* or self-deprecation: *hey, could you look out for my mind when you take me back to the hotel, because I think I just lost it.*

By the time Roma pulls to the curb and kills the engine, I've decided on sincerity. I reach for the strap of my helmet, ready to tell him how much I enjoyed the ride. I imagine his chivalrous response and my satisfaction when I walk away without a backward glance. But that's not what happens. What happens is that Roma dismounts and, wordlessly, leaves me perched on the listing motorcycle.

I watch him walk up to a man loitering in the door of an Italian restaurant. The sign reads SAN SOLE, but it looks sunless inside. The man has bloodshot eyes and a toothpick rolling across his lips. He exudes the brutal competence that comes only from bringing police-state training to the private sector. He's bigger than Roma, but less comfortable in his skin. They slap hands. Roma flips up his visor and speaks. I can't hear anything over the jackhammers tearing up the street. The other man looks over at me and nods. He pulls the toothpick from his mouth and opens the door of the restaurant. It appears to be my cue.

I'm on my feet. Roma is walking back toward me. There's no trace of familiarity in his eyes. The rest of his face is hidden, protected. He looks less like a hot guy. More like a henchman. I hand him the helmet, and I'm almost furious, but he touches my arm.

"I'll be seeing you," he says.

We don't say it that way in Russian.

MY EYES TAKE A moment to adjust to the darkness inside. A hostess in a tight dress leads me to a table in the corner where an elderly man in a black jacket and shirt with no tie is already seated. I want to laugh. I've seen the American movies. The godfathers who hold court with their backs to the wall, their eyes on the entrance, their guns close to their chests. But it's not quite as funny to live such a scene *in* America.

He looks up over narrow spectacles and rises to greet me. He smiles kindly, but doesn't overplay it. He doesn't take my hand or even my long jacket, which is now flecked with the mud of Second Avenue roadwork. He has bread crumbs on his chest; the glass of wine before him is half drunk. He's old, but how old? Floppy salt-and-pepper hair tucked behind his ears suggests sixty. His dark, deeply lined face says older. I'm trying to remember what time it is. And why it should be the hour to invite a teenager to dinner.

"Sit, *dorogaya*. Take a load off," he says. "I hope Roma drove safely? Behaved himself? I told him to be civil. He sometimes forgets his, shall we say, social skills."

I don't answer. I sit. A waiter appears.

"Bring my friend here a bottle of Perrier, a plate of pasta and—what else, Lana, dear? Far be it from me to order for you, but I do know a thing or two about dancer diets. Carbs, lots of them. But maybe also a salad? Lamb chops, *nu*?"

"I'll have Bolognese, please," I tell the waiter in my practiced English. "Flat mineral water. No gas. No ice."

"A glass of wine perhaps?" suggests Georgi, sticking to Russian.

I shake my head.

"I can tell already that you are a young lady of tremendous sagacity," he says once the waiter has left. "I'm delighted. Since one never knows how misguided one's anticipations might be. Particularly in long-awaited introductions."

His Russian is old-fashioned. Not the neglected ease of Roma's last-generation Russian, but deliberately charming. Like a handcrafted artifact. I'm not sure whether to believe his careful speech or his careless dress. Is he a sloth or a shark, or both?

"Who are you?"

"I am Georgi Levshik. A businessman, a patron of the arts, a lover of the Bolshoi."

Bozhe, another big-spending sycophant. Why did I cross New York to meet with someone I would have avoided like the plague back home?

"And I am also your mother's closest friend. Though she probably doesn't think so."

I let my wide eyes convey doubt, not the shock that he has just given me. I let them dispute the notion that he, a disheveled but articulate businessman, is Marina's closest friend.

"How do you know my mother?" I ask. "From here? Or from Moscow?"

"*Da.* From New York. And from Moscow."

"And yet, she has never mentioned you. To me."

Georgi swirls his wine until it paints the sides of the glass pink.

"Never mentioned me, her Dyadya Gosha." He seems to be talking to himself.

I open my mouth to clarify what he means by *dyadya*—uncle. Does my mother really have an uncle that she has never mentioned? Why not? She rarely speaks of her father and never of her mother. I could have a handful of uncles and aunts sprinkled between New York and Moscow, for all I know. None of whom will ever be my *dyadya* nor my *tyotya*. Blood is not always stronger than water. Sometimes it evaporates.

"Your mother never was one to discuss her friends," he says. "Or her family. She has so few of either."

He raises his eyes to mine. I hold them. But I drop the question of what sort of "Uncle Gosha" this man has been to my mother—the ambiguities of *dyadya* are too uncomfortable. I'll pull at another curtain for now.

"What sort of business are you engaged in?" I ask.

"The usual business that men like me, dumped at the racetrack without a horse, engage in."

He pauses to allow the waiter to serve us and flourish his extra-long pepper grinder over the table.

"I made some wild bets that paid off. Now I meet people, I connect people, I make money. I like to spend that money, invest it. In people I care about. In things that I care for. The arts, for example. I am a considerable donor to the Bolshoi, though I like to keep my name out of it. Except, of course, when it comes to you. I want you, Lana, to know my name."

Something clicks. *Vartukh says you have a patron.* And now I know his name.

"And how about Pavel Vartukh? Does he know your name, Mr. Levshik? Does he know that I'm here with you? Is that why your young minion out there showed up just as I left rehearsal? Is this late lunch, early dinner my consolation prize?"

He drops his napkin and raises his hands, as if my bitterness has reminded him of something marvelous. "Lana! My congratulations, *dorogaya*!" He claps his hands together. "It should have been the first thing out of my mouth. Damn thoughtless! Let's raise a glass to your New York debut. And at Lincoln Center, by God! Well, I can't tell you how very proud I am, Lana. Honestly. This . . . this is almost as wonderful as if . . ."

He stops. Delight fades. I see something cross his face like a shadow. I've seen it before on my mother's face. Remorse. Regret.

I don't raise my glass. I consider setting him straight. The congratulatory toast is far from its mark. My debut is an anticlimax, but he appears not to know that I am nothing more than a benchwarmer. Or maybe he doesn't care. He has already moved on (or back) . . . to my mother.

"It was a terrible blow to me," he says, his lips still on the rim of the glass. "Your mother leaving the ballet. She had so much talent. Such a waste."

"That's not a kind thing to say to her daughter," I reply. "It is, after all, rather my fault."

"Your fault?" he asks. "You presume too much."

"Well, I don't mean I got her pregnant, of course. But nonetheless . . ."

He frowns and puts the wine glass down. He picks up his fork, puts it back down. "I think perhaps, you don't have the full story," he says.

"That's for damn sure."

There is a clatter from the kitchen. I glance up and see eyes in the porthole of the swinging door. They disappear quickly. Someone turns down the lights and turns up the background music. Georgi appears not to notice.

I lean across the table and speak. "I think that it is you who presume too much, Georgi Levshik. I didn't have to come here, you know. Bolshoi patron or no, old acquaintance or no, you have no claim on me."

He pulls his bottom lip with a thumb and forefinger, waiting.

"Or do you?" I continue. "Do you want to make a claim?"

He doesn't rise to the bait.

I feel a wave of fatigue slip over my head. I feel labored, doomed, like I am breathing underwater. "I'd like you to cut to the chase. I am on tour. I am on a schedule. I am on the clock."

"And you are under suspicion," he says simply.

That fatigue vanishes. It is gone. It's running scared.

"When did you find out I was in New York?" I demand. "If my mother didn't tell you, you shouldn't know. I was a last-minute addition."

"And a last-minute joyful surprise for me."

Now I'm sure. He's not nobody. He's been there all along. But how long is "all along." The last year? The last eighteen? From the moment I was conceived? Dear God, is he . . . ?

"Who are you?" My voice is husky. Hating. *Please, not him.*

"I was the best man at your grandparents' wedding," Georgi says. "We vacationed together every summer in the Baltics. Me and Vitya served in the army, near Tver. And then came your mother. The apple of her daddy's eye. You know, I took Marya to kindergarten every day for two years. Picked her up, too, at two o'clock, and we took the tram home down Leninskie Hills. Must have been between nannies. And me? Between wives I suspect. So there we were. Marya and her Dyadya Gosha. Sitting on my knee since, what, 1968?"

Almost half a century.

I fold my napkin over my half-eaten dish and clear my throat. "That was a long time ago. And the fact that you have lots of tales about my grandparents tells me nothing, since I actually know very little about my grandparents."

He raises his eyebrows. Then he sighs. "Well, yes, I could see how that would be the case. So you see, we have much to discuss."

Georgi picks up his wineglass. It is empty. His eyes flick up for the waiter but then focus on me. It's just a moment, but I read his priorities. If our dinner is not to be pleasant, then it can still be productive.

I stand. "I don't think so. I think we have nothing to discuss. I'm leaving."

He stands, too, and grips my arm. Too hard.

"I understand you are conflicted," he says, his voice low. "Perhaps I misplayed this, our first meeting. I do, sometimes, misstep. Of course you are free to go, Lana. But hear me out."

His grip tightens. I'm suddenly aware that there is no one else in the restaurant. Just me and this Dyadya Gosha.

"I have always, and will always, do what's best for you and your mother. Marina knows that. When you were born she told me that what was best for her was to break her ties with me. And I respected that. But you are your own person, Lana. You must make your own choices. I stand ready, as always, to demonstrate my devotion to the Dukovskaya family. And as you are in my town now, you should expect that I have more say in the matter than I did before you arrived."

I cannot even begin to think of a response. I just want him to let go of my arm. His voice has lost its polish, its gentility. It's the voice of authority. He is, yes, a boss. A shark. His eyes are hard, but I see emotion play his face. Reading mine, he releases me. I hold my breath, struggling not to betray my relief.

"You must decide whether or not to tell your mother that you have met me," he says. Now he sounds formal. "We have been out of touch for so long, I don't know how she will react. Whatever she has chosen to remember of me . . . whatever I have done that she cannot forgive. These are things that I will work all my life to rectify. I may never have her love back. But maybe, I will once again hear her say thank you."

He pulls a yellow manila envelope from inside his jacket and puts it in my hand.

"I can see you have doubts. These are the only bona fides that should matter to you. I will fetch you when you have examined them."

I race from the restaurant. But I think: Another goddamn envelope in place of a goodbye.

BONA FIDES, HE HAD said. Good faith.

The words swim in my head as I stare at the small pile I've dumped onto my lap. The taxi swerves and the contents of Georgi Levshik's envelope spill onto the floor, along with my composure.

"Stop the car!" I shout. "Stop. Please. Here. I want out."

The driver shoots me a look in the rearview mirror. He seems lost here, like me. He's dark complected. Certain Russian skinheads might try to run him down with a motorcycle. I just want out of his cab. His eyes are surprised but not stupid. Still, we are equally primitive in our English. Conversation is not an option.

"Yes. I want out," I repeat.

He pulls over slowly. I shove money through the partition between us and gather the precious evidence of Georgi's "good faith" from the floor. Then I grab my black dance bag and clamber out of the cab.

My haste makes me clumsy. I scan Central Park, stretching the whole length of Fifth Avenue. I lurch back inside its walls, following a path past children whining for ice cream and cyclists wrapped in Lycra. I climb a steep hill to a stone outcrop. The landscape below me is in bloom. I try to inhale it. I try to breathe spring, to embrace the season of revelations and the sudden appearance of what we knew was there all along. But I can't quite catch my breath.

I take a seat on the rock and force my clenched fist to let go of Georgi's bona fides. I spread them in front of me. They show me—in hues of a faded era, in small undigitized, low-resolution squares—answers to questions I've almost stopped asking.

There are two photos, a booklet, and a creased piece of paper covered entirely in slightly out-of-control blue ink.

I pick up one of the snapshots first. A wedding banquet from last century. Dated by the details: the striped wallpaper; the brand of vodka on the table; the bouncy curls of the head blocking the camera's lower range; the enormous stacked cake placed just so in the center of a tablecloth studded with emblems of the cosmos.

This first photo is from the 1960s. We had just put a man in space, and his glorious heroic feats were celebrated in every corner of the Soviet Union. Even at this wedding banquet. The bride, laughing and effortlessly beautiful, is in long sleeves and a short skirt. The groom wears an enormous bow tie and oversize glasses. They are both looking away from the laden table at the man standing between them. He is caught in mid gesture, as if conducting an orchestra of ceremony and camaraderie.

I peer more closely at the ebullient face and the hands frozen in a blur of motion, and I recognize Georgi Levshik.

The next photo is more faded. One corner is erased

entirely. I imagine the triangular tab that anchored it in a spiral album for decades until it was plucked from an album. It shows the same three—the couple that must be my grandparents—together with Dyadya Gosha. The two men flank the lady, who is hatless and flushed. They surge arm in arm toward the camera, part of a crowd that could be a Party demonstration, a patriotic parade, or perhaps a still from a propaganda film celebrating the vigors of Soviet youth. I hear my own childish voice: "*A tvoya mama krasivaya byla?*" Was your mother pretty? And Marina's assurance: "*Izumitel'no krasivaya.*" Fantastically so.

I put down the photo and pick up the booklet. It's a playbill from the Bolshoi Ballet, though I would hardly recognize it as such, three skimpy pages printed on cheap paper and sloppily stapled. It's a far cry from the glossy programs of today, with their pages of corporate sponsors and absurd advertisements for luxury cars and watches. But it's affixed with the Bolshoi logo and emblazoned in the proudly proletarian logotype of all Soviet spectacles:

MARCH 25, 1965. PREMIERE PRESENTATION:
THE RITE OF SPRING
MUSIC BY IGOR STRAVINSKY

I'm so struck by the coincidence that I almost don't notice the smaller print below.

Featuring Svetlana Dukovskaya as the Chosen One

Sure enough, when I turn the page I am greeted by the long-haired bride, my mother's mother. For a minute I can't focus. I can't see anything before me. Not the tree limbs dancing. Not the clouds scudding between bud-tipped branches. Not even the grainy image of Svetlana Dukovskaya, prima ballerina of the Bolshoi Ballet.

No, goddamn it, I didn't know.

What did I know? I knew that my grandmother was named Svetlana and that I am named for her.

And now I know she was the Chosen One. Who never returned to my mother.

I sit back and hold my swimming head in my hands. This information presents as many questions as answers. It's not just my mother who has been silent about this. It's everyone. No one—not Anna Arkhipova, not Pavel Vartukh, not even Ludmila Kirilovna, my tutor who has been at the Ballet since, well, probably since we sent our man into space—has hinted that I am a third-generation Dukovskaya at the Bolshoi Theatre.

I want to yell at the playbill. Force it to reveal more than the amateurish touched-up portrait, the brief history of *The Rite of Spring* as a "magisterial expression of the role of the collective in the natural world and the triumph of humanity over idolatry."

Instead, I pick up the last of the envelope's contents, this folded paper scrawled in blue ink.

In a moment I have forgotten my mysterious grandmother, for here is a confession from my mysterious mother.

The first line reads:

Dear Gosha,
    I'm not ready to admit that you were right.

The last line reads:

With love,
Marya

And in between, tucked in the fold of the single page is another photograph. I pick it up and study the way the man balances a large summer melon and a tanned, serious girl in the same expansive embrace. It's the third picture I've seen of the young Georgi Levshik. It's the second picture I've seen of the young Marina Dukovskaya. But in this one, unlike the picture that hangs in the Juilliard School, I can see her face. It is strong. It is confident. If I didn't recognize myself in her face, I would not know it was my mother. I run a finger over her long tan legs and smile at the prim braids pinned on top of her head. My heart wants to break for my Marya, who wears her Dyadya Gosha's arm like a dress-up cape.

I think, *Who was he to her?*

I think, *She's not sitting on his knee, whatever he wants to remember.*

EIGHT
THE SKELETON IN THE CLOSET

The good thing about the bomb that Georgi's bona fides have dropped on me is that my other personal problems have been laid waste. For example, I haven't given a single thought to Daniela since yesterday afternoon. Tonight, my company takes the stage at Lincoln Center without me, and I'm not even upset. No, I've got other things on my mind.

Or at least that's what I tell Nina.

She suggests a movie. I roll my eyes.

"Just to get your mind off things," she explains.

"Neen," I say, "if my mind gets any further 'off,' you're going to have to institutionalize me."

I had confided in her. Last night after a slow walk home from my Central Park outcrop. Not about everything. I told her that I got a hold of this stuff from some fan of mine, a cute boy on a motorcycle who spoke Russian. I didn't tell Nina that I had a secret meeting with an older man who might be my grandfather's brother, or my grandmother's paramour, or my mother's sugar daddy or even my . . . I don't want to think that. Even if it's something that more than a decade of secrecy has primed me to suspect. Something that digs like the photo of my pubescent, long-legged Marina in the arms of a doting but devilish Dyadya Gosha.

Dyadya, I tell myself. *Not Papa.*

Patron, I know almost certainly.

Still, I said nothing about Georgi to Nina. I just handed her the old program. I thought that she might have something to add. After all, it must have been the same Danse Sacrale that Vartukh was coaching her for—the Svetlana Variation.

"What a crazy thing," she had breathed, flipping through the program for clues. "Where do you think that boy got ahold of this stuff?"

I'd shrugged.

"You know, I didn't really pay attention to Pavel when he told me about this Svetlana Variation. I mean, it seemed like ancient history. Basically, he said there was no written record of the choreography and no tapes of a live performance. At the time I didn't think anything of it, but now . . . I mean, it's weird. Like . . ."

I knew what she was thinking. Like it wasn't just the Svetlana Variation that had disappeared. Svetlana herself had disappeared, too.

"And look how much she looks like your mother. What does Marina say?" she had asked, her eyes wide.

I told her that Marina had basically disappeared, too.

With a "whatever" shrug. Like, you know, my mother is always dropping off the grid. Marina and her technophobia, ha ha. I tried to believe it.

"This must be what they meant by a favor to your mother, though, no?" Nina had asked, handing the program back to me. "A sentimental gesture."

Neither of us had stated the obvious. That it was Nina who had been trained to dance Svetlana's variation. That I didn't even know the steps. That it was a terribly cruel gesture, not sentimental at all.

LATER, WHEN THE GIRLS were all asleep, the darker thoughts surfaced. I lay in bed thinking of Svetlana as the Chosen One—hunted by her elders until she disappeared.

Russia, you see, is good at making people disappear. For a long period (like, all of the twentieth century, when Svetlana Dukovskaya lived and danced and disappeared) lots of other Russians disappeared, too. From their families or from their workplaces or from their apartment blocks. And sometimes they vanished from history. If you were a bigwig in the Communist Party, or a general, or some famous scientist, cosmonaut, writer—whatever—there was a good chance that one fine morning your name would be erased and your face scrubbed from the annals. Gone. Poof.

But ballerinas? I had never heard of a Bolshoi ballerina being forced into oblivion. Though, I guess that's the point. That, after all, is a successful disappearance: one that your own flesh and blood don't notice.

The more I lay there thinking about what might have happened to Svetlana, the more I sweated. Because Russia is Russia. Even without the Soviets and the Communists and the KGB secret police, Russia is still a country that doesn't think twice about making certain types disappear. The ones who clamor for justice. The ones who dig up dirt and put it on the Internet. The activists, the bloggers, the whistle-blowers. The ones who point fingers at the Kremlin and yell, *Vori!* Stop, thief!

I've mentioned that the Bolshoi, Russia's crown jewel, is just across the square from the Kremlin, right?

I've mentioned that I'm a loudmouth? A whistle-blower? A clamorer? Also, a Bolshoi ballerina. A Dukovskaya.

I tossed and turned and wondered. *Am I supposed to disappear, too? Is that what I've been chosen for?*

The moon was already setting when I finally crawled out of bed and read again the letter my mother wrote in Moscow nearly twenty years ago and sent to Georgi in New York.

Dear Gosha,

I'm not ready to admit that you were right.

It's all still too fresh. The records are still locked up. Glasnost—that brief crack of light—has been filled back up. Nobody cares about an old ballerina, even one that went from Artist of the People to Enemy of the People overnight. It's a scandal! And I won't take no for an answer. But the problem is, I have so little time. I'm rehearsing for Sleeping Beauty, *and the baby takes all my free time.*

But I will find her, Gosha. I owe it to my daughter to find my mother. It's her legacy!

> *With love,*
> *Marya*

PS. Danilov has hinted I will move out of the corps by spring. Imagine! I might dance Dulcinea on the Bolshoi stage. You will have to come for that, Gosha—no excuses!

PPS. Don't write me again about B. I've made my decision. I want this more than I want love.

I sat a long time in the moonlight of the air shaft, wondering what to make of this girl. Who is this Marya with her exclamation points and determination and serial postscripts? PS? PPS? Is this really my mother? The girl who *won't take no for an answer*! The one who rocked me to sleep at night thinking *it's her legacy*! And what to make of this rejection of B.? This rejection of love?

That's when I started crying. When I recognized that my mother had gambled her dreams and lost. She wanted something more than love. She got neither. *My dreams told me I would be alone.*

I slid the letter back into the envelope, right beside the one she wrote to me, and tucked both of them in the bottom of my suitcase. Then I went to sleep, wondering what Georgi Levshik had done to lose my mother's trust.

• • •

NOW, RESTED BUT UNSETTLED and not taking the stage tonight, I've got more questions. I'm pacing our too-small room, with its discrete funk of girls and take-out food. Nina is painting her toenails and stealing glances at me. "Why don't you ask Pavel? He must know something. He's the one who called it the Svetlana Variation."

I nod. She's right of course. *We've seen it, Lana. We've already seen your Danse Sacrale.*

I grab my phone and my dance bag. I pull on my jacket and flip the collar. I lean on the bed to plant a kiss on Nina's cheek. She *tsks*—I've smudged the fresh layer of polish on her big toe. Like it matters. Dancers' feet are hideous beyond help.

"I'll be backstage by five thirty to help you get ready," I promise, and then I'm out the door.

I DON'T FIND VARTUKH in his hotel room. I don't find him in the restaurant or in the coffee shop or out front smoking with the three prettiest primas in their over-sized superstar designer sunglasses.

"Come shopping, Lana?" asks one of them, the most mannered. A taxi slides up to let them in. I decline and they're gone, off to spend their five hours of downtime like normal people.

I look left toward Lincoln Center and right toward the vanishing point of upper Broadway. I plug earbuds into my phone and cue music that has begun to make sense. Songs about dreams so real. *All the unknown dying or dead keep showing up in my dreams.*

Then I stride north into unfamiliar territory. I untie the sash of my long jacket and let it blow in my wake. I'm surprised when the sound of a motorcycle speeding past makes me walk different. Sexy.

And then something more surprising. Pavel Vartukh sitting on the other side of a plate-glass window. Pavel Vartukh knocking on the chipped paint that reads NIGHT DIVE. Pavel Vartukh beckoning me. I pull out my earphones and enter the dank air of a saloon at midday.

I've seen our artistic director tipsy once or twice. It's usually an occasion for hands a bit too low on the back, a nuzzle behind the ear. A suggestive joke. Dancers my age are expected to respond with a blush and light push. More senior dancers know to expect a straightforward proposition. The smartest keep sober and let alcohol convince our artistic director that his attentions have been met with more fervor than fact.

But that's not what is going on here in Night Dive. Here he is alone, bereft, utterly unamorous. Pavel Vartukh is drunk. I take a stool next to him and order a club soda. He shoots back a whiskey and looks at me with bloodshot eyes.

"You're going to be in bad shape for the opening," I say, pushing the club soda toward him.

"Doesn't matter," he slurs. "S'not my show anymore."

"Whose is it?"

He wipes his mouth with the back of his hand.

"What'uld you say if I told you it was the Dukovskaya show?"

"I would say you are not being any more honest with me than you have been for the past three days."

Pavel Vartukh orders another shot of whiskey and tells me all sorts of things. About his first tour, about his first solo, about his first critical review, about the first dancer he ever screwed—

I cut him off. I ask him if the solo is on the program. He laughs and says: "Yeah, sure, the program is on solo. Automatic. Autopilot drive. No two-man operation, this program. A one-man show. One woman. One wo-man."

I ask him if it was his choice to bring me to New York.

"I made that 'choice,' Lana, with the same gun to my head that Anna held on you," he answers.

"I don't know what you mean. What does Anna have on me?"

"On me. On you. Anna, Anya, Anyushka," he mumbles. "Wrapped around my neck."

"Pavel Artemovich, please focus." I take the glass from him, glare at the hovering bartender.

"S'not mine," he mutters. "I've lost control of the ballet. She's in charge. She's gonna . . . gonna put you onstage and . . . gonna bring you down."

It's good he's not sober. Those words would be scary sober. But now, it's *polniy bred*. Complete bullshit. Drunken blathering. I try another direction.

"You knew my mother, Pavel?"

He leans back, almost falls off his stool. "Pretty thing, Marina. But skittish."

"Did she ask for me to be included on the tour?" I prod. "Did she come to you and ask that you bring me?"

He smirks. He holds his hand up for the bartender. I smack it down. He's so drunk he doesn't notice.

"Did she?"

"Marina, Marya. Marinka Kalinka." Vartukh promises to lose himself in another tongue twister of nicknames.

I press on. "Why the selection of Danse Sacrale? Why is it in honor of my mother? Did you know my grandmother? Svetlana?"

He finally looks at me, his face is blank.

"Never heard of her."

There's a roar from the other end of the bar, closer to the television with its baseball game. When I turn back to Pavel he appears to be half asleep.

"*Pozor*," I hiss. "Aren't you ashamed? How can you call yourself a director? You're pathetic. In more ways than I ever knew."

He snorts. "Many revelations abroad, no? T's always a surprise, what comes to light when you're outta the Bolshoi's . . ." He hiccups. "Shadow."

I study him, swaying on his stool.

"Do you know a man named Georgi Levshik?" I ask.

That's when he starts laughing. Crazy, unhinged laughing.

"Man with bad fucking aim," he cackles as I pay the bill, flag a cab and hold him upright for the two-minute drive back to the hotel. "Man with terrible fucking aim."

But when I've finally managed to deposit our artistic

director safely in his room, without anyone from the company witnessing the mess that he has become, Vartukh stops laughing. He sits up on the bed and says: "Svetlana?"

"Yes," I say. "Svetlana Dukovskaya, prima ballerina. She danced the Chosen One once upon a time."

He nods his head in something like sympathy. "If you've got a skeleton in your closet, Lana . . . you had better teach it to dance."

THOUGH IT IS MOSTLY a sweaty swamp of sounds, *The Rite of Spring* does have a message. It has a simple story: a gathering; a service; a realization; a ritual. By which I mean a murder.

I'm not a musicologist or anything, but I do know that this is a piece that you have to understand. It's not enough to just let it "possess" you, which is what most dancers will say about their preparation for the ballet. If I've heard it once, I've heard it a million times: *You have to let the passions, the emotions, possess you . . . and fill your soul with this . . . primitive energy.*

It's true, okay. But lazy. It's a cliché. There's more to it. You can't be possessed by cacophony. You can't be entranced by chaos. It's the directives underneath the clamor that you have to hear. It's no different from any musical acquired taste. Even metal, or trance. Or Rihanna, for that matter. The rhythm is the direction. And something else. Something I don't have a word for, but I'd sooner just remain at a loss for words than write it off as "passion" or "raw power" or certainly not "emotion." Something discoverable. Something you can follow to the truth.

I'm lacing on my shoes in the fourth-floor studio that the Juilliard security guy kindly opened up for me. "Don't do anything I wouldn't." He had winked. I wondered if that applied to *grand jetés*.

I cue the music to the beginning of the ballet . . . well before the Danse Sacrale.

The haunted bassoon opens a path through the woods into a clearing. The other instruments follow, individually and in pairs, talking among themselves. It sounds to some like an orchestra warming up. But it is not. It's a people filling the glade. Falling into lockstep, synching their pagan expressions, sharpening their spears. Now the heavy orchestral blare from some volcanic god. Then the sudden raucous flurry of the piccolos—a startled flight of birds.

They're so fast, the transitions in the piece.

I'm up on my feet, running away from the frantic woodwinds, checking each corner of the studio for refuge from this scary Spring. I feel the tingle of sweat, the confidence of my muscles. My body is grateful for anything Stravinsky wants to throw at it. Layer upon layer of rhythm have their way with me. I relish it. And then, in a moment of silence, I think of my mother on the stage with me that day. The day of my departure. I think of how she harmonized my strength with her meekness.

One chosen for sacrifice, her body had said, *can only escape by hiding her soul.*

I stop dancing and walk slowly to the stereo to cue

the recording of the finale: the solo. As I do, I catch a
glimpse in the mirror of the studio door opening. My
body floods with fresh heat, recognizing that it's Roma,
and recognizing my response—that I'm going to pretend
not to notice his intrusion. He sits in a small folding
chair by the door. I hit PLAY.

There is no mercy as it begins. The music is a circle
of arrows and knives that first I dodge and then I deflect
with unrestrained arms, flexed wrists, and the legs of
a martial artist. I win this round, and the trumpets are
angry. They call for round two. The beat is relentless. It
circles and circles, like a tightening noose. My toes are
anchors . . . screws in the spring soil, and my body a
drill. I'm building my own sacrificial altar and the drums
are directing where to lay the beams. I've lost the rapid
frappé skips that I had honed just days ago and replace
them with improvised jumps—in second position, in a
contraction . . . and then higher and more frightened, as
my head touches my knees. For the first time I hear in
the strings of the violins and cellos, the ropes that will
bind me to my sacrificial altar.

Still jumping as if —well, yes, "possessed"—I force
myself to hear, somewhere outside of this entrapment, the
sound of that lovely bassoon. The first call of nature.
The sound of a new moon that will hide, with its light-
lessness, my secret place. The place I will hide my soul.

I embrace the eclectic swarm of the music. I dance
with the small night watchers, with the insects and
birds. I leap right into the center of the ring of hunt-
ers, the louts in animal skins. I bare my breast to the

elders, the shrieking dervishes that have replaced the violins. And then I lie down on the altar, feel the pulse of its kettledrum base, and I die.

The clouds part. The sun pierces the western window.

Roma stands, the chair clatters. My soul cheers in the silence that follows. I lie motionless on the floor. A skeleton.

And one hell of a dancer.

ROMA'S BLUE EYES ARE grey in the studio. He lowers them, done with what he has to say. I was listening, but I'm not sure what he said. Not exactly. Only that whatever he said about my dancing was just right. It was not too much. It was not too little. And it was surprising. It told me that this boy knows something about ballet and he knows something about me . . . and that, maybe, he knew these things even before he saw them here in this studio.

But I don't acknowledge that. Instead I say, "Are you fucking stalking me, Roma?"

And he reads that correctly, too. He says, "Yes, Lana, I am." He reaches down and hands me a small towel from my bag. "It's my job."

I take the towel. I wipe the sweat from my neck. I do a slow lap of the studio, letting my breath slow.

"Who is this Levshik? Why should I trust him?" I ask from across the room. "No—wait. I know who he says he is. And I know why he thinks I should trust him." I clear my throat and start again. "What I want to know is: Who is Georgi Levshik to you?"

He raises his eyes, surprised to be asked.

"Why do you trust him?" I clarify.

"He's my boss," he says, an answer too wise and so naïve. It's dangerous. "I trust him because I do not work for people I don't trust."

It's an odd assurance. But there's another question that bothers me more, and I can't ask it. I can acknowledge that Roma, a stranger, knows things about Georgi Levshik that I don't know. But I can't ask if he knows things about me that I don't. I won't ask if he knows who my father is.

Instead, I throw a softball. "Is he a criminal?"

"You know the answer. He's a businessman. An old Soviet. An ex-Sovok. A self-made American. A philanthropist. You know exactly what he is. A rich man with rich tastes and many resources. He breaks the rules that hurt the fewest. He plays the games that benefit the most. And by 'most'—that is a vague quantifiable. The most what? Well . . . that depends on the stakes."

This, too, is somehow an answer that reassures me. Roma doesn't frighten me. Roma is no thug. He says things like "vague quantifiable." He is under orders, but also under control.

Now he rubs the back of his neck. "My boss is also extremely loyal."

"That's a strange compliment for a flunky to pay a gangster."

He doesn't smile or even blink. "Look, Lana. You should trust him." He's not moved a centimeter closer, but I feel the space between us diminish. "You trust me. I trust him. Associative property."

"So you're a mathematician as well as a toady," I say. "And what makes you think I trust you?"

"The fact that you let me see you dance."

I turn my back so he can't see what he has done to me.

"What time is it?" I ask. "I need to be backstage at the theater by five thirty."

"You have an hour."

"I need to change," I say. "Could you wait outside?"

"Sure. I'll be on the street."

He steps out and I strip the spring forest from my body and pull on blue jeans, a silk blouse, and my Converse sneakers. I'm not performing anymore. I can look good on my own terms. And yes, I check the mirror to make sure I do.

Outside Roma is watching a cluster of girls in short dresses. Their long necks and bunheads signal that they are of my breed, but if they are swans, I'm a kamikaze bird of prey. They are tossing smiles at him like rose petals; I've just fired bullets at him. They flirt for him; I've very nearly stripped for him.

He turns and looks at me, and I can see the other girls vanish from his vision.

"So," I say.

"So," he says.

"So Georgi sent you, I presume. Please tell him that tonight is opening night and I am not available just now. I've reviewed the things he gave—"

"He didn't."

"Didn't?"

"Didn't send me. I mean, he would have. He will. He'll be in the audience tonight, certainly, and I'm sure he is hoping that you will have time for him afterward. But that's later."

"Later. And now? Now you were what, just passing by?"

"I was outside the hotel. I saw you get out of a taxi with Pavel Vartukh."

I shake my head. It's sick. This guy is my shadow and I'm almost flattered.

"Vartukh. So you know who he is, too? Georgi's educated you?"

He doesn't answer that.

"It didn't look so good," he mutters.

I remember Vartukh staggering from the cab, nearly pulling me into the potted plant at the door and I laugh, mirthlessly. "I have a habit of getting into these situations that look bad."

A stupid amount of time passes. Enough time to make it obvious that I haven't walked away from him.

"I better go," I say.

"Listen."

I sling my bag from one shoulder to the other. I'm listening.

"I get the feeling that you're here, in New York, not just to dance. I get the feeling you're here to discover something."

"I'm here to dance," I answer too quickly. "It's your boss who's decided to turn it into some sort of epiphany. Some sort of reunion that, frankly, I never asked for."

Lies. Half lies. I didn't ask for a reunion, but don't I

want one? And yes—I came to New York to dance, but didn't I know that I wouldn't?

"I'm here to dance," I say again, but the words are empty.

He nods and squints into the distance. "Okay."

I'm still standing on the sidewalk. Why am I still standing on the sidewalk?

"Well. It's not my business," he says finally. "But there are ways to find your way without asking Georgi for directions."

"Speak plainly." My voice is a whisper.

He pivots and points across the street.

"That's the Lincoln Center Library for the Performing Arts," he says.

I follow his finger. There's a glass double door at street level below the main plaza. It's fifty feet from the passage that leads to the Met's stage door, but he might as well be pointing to Novodevichy Cemetery, it seems such an unlikely destination for me right now.

"You have forty-five minutes," he says. "That's valuable time."

I feel a wave of panic, followed by fatigue. A scream becoming a yawn.

"Svetlana Dukovskaya?" I say.

"Yes. And also . . . Benjamin Frame."

"Benjamin Frame . . ." I repeat.

"That's right."

I'm still standing there. I smell something. Grass. Lilac. How can that be? On the corner of Tenth Avenue and 65th Street.

"I can come with you."

He sees me refuse to trust him.

"But . . . I should probably move my bike. It's illegally parked."

I nod.

"So I guess I'll see you after . . ."

I nod again.

He turns to go.

"Thank you," I say.

"Save your thanks," he says.

I watch him go. My genie in the bottle. My genie on wheels.

A LIBRARIAN DIRECTS ME to a computer with an online catalog. In thirty seconds I've confirmed that my ignorance is deep. Svetlana Dukovskaya has several entries: recorded performances of; monographs including; iconography, ephemera; programs; tours; Soviet career; awards and commendations: People's Artist of the USSR.

Yes. Just as Marina's letter indicated, my grandmother wasn't just a prima. She was an Artist of the People. The highest commendation in the Soviet Ministry of Culture. They know that here in America. They know about Svetlana Dukovskaya. They know about my grandmother, and I do not.

My palms are slick. Remember what I said? About generals and big shots? They are the ones who disappeared. The ones whose absence required that the presses worked overtime to write new histories and shred the old ones. I wonder for a minute how Georgi's old Bolshoi program made it out. I wonder again if the people I work with every day know about this woman. I wonder what she must have done to make them plead ignorance. Worse— to make her own daughter hide her.

I struggle with the catalog and its cross-references and annotations. I click on links and lose my way. Here are DVDs of the "Stars of the Bolshoi." Here are biographies of Ulanova and Bessmertnova, histories of the golden era of the Bolshoi, reference works on the choreography of Balanchine, Vaganova, Danilov. Danilov—Vartukh's legendary predecessor. Another click and I'm back in the 1920s with Nijinsky and his *Rite of Spring*.

I start over. I type in Svetlana Dukovskaya. Death.

Up pops a bomb: "Did the Soviet Union's greatest bal-lerina commit suicide?" *Dance Magazine*, March 1983.

And then: obituaries.

I scramble up from the monitor and cross over to the woman sitting at a desk opposite behind a plaque that reads REFERENCE LIBRARIAN. She hands me a pack of slips in triplicate and a blunt pencil. She shows me all the other slips in her inbox.

"Call number, address, title, publication, volume . . ." she says, and then sees the dismay on my face.

She comes out from behind the desk and hovers over the computer with me. I point, she writes. Then she says that it will take time, that the article from 1983 is only available on microfiche. She points to another end of the room where ancient film readers sit black and silent like shrunken mausoleums for tiny dead ballerinas.

"How long?" I ask.

"Twenty minutes," she says.

I glance at the clock: 5:10. "Twenty?" I gasp.

The librarian puts her finger to her lips.

I sit back down at the catalog and close my eyes. I fish the name from Roma's lips: *Benjamin Frame.* Well. What the hell.

I sit up and type. There are many pages of results. They read like a scholarly bibliography: Structural Hearing: Tonal Coherence in Music; Visibility and Voice Leading; Counterpoint and Instrumentation. All three of those in six more languages. Recordings, dozens of them. I scroll, scroll. At the top of the third page: "How Not to Hear *The Rite of Spring*: Theories and Recordings," Frame, Benjamin, PhD. *Nauchnyi Vestnik: The Quarterly Journal of Moscow State Conservatory 22,* January 1993. And after that: "Automated Rhythm and the Holy Fool: Modularity and the Metaphysical in Stravinsky's Ballets," *Acta Musicologica,* Vol 72, pp 25–29.

So what? What does Benjamin Frame have to tell me about my Danse Sacrale?

I click on his name. The catalog gives me this: Russian American music scholar and composer. (1964–)

Okay. So he is alive. Or at least not dead. Though the absence of a second date, I realize, should not be taken too literally. Especially when it's not written in stone in Novodevichy Cemetery.

I pull out my phone and dial Marina's number. I get a busy signal, the fast kind. The kind that says it's not

Marina that is occupied. It is everything between me and her. I plug the earbuds in. I close my eyes and cue up my theme song: *Anyone not dying is dead.*

Shut up.

Carry on.

The librarian is back with a small stack of magazines. *Time* magazine, *Dance Magazine, Ballet Today.* They are dated 1999. The microfiche from 1983 is curled on top like a snail.

"Would you like help with the microfiche first?" she asks.

"Please."

I follow her across the room to where she threads the film through the complex mechanics of one of the bulky machines. She hits a button and the wheels whirl. I think of piccolos, drums and screams. A flick of the wrist and the wheels and the black-and-white images they project slow down. I see Svetlana slide beyond the upper reach of the screen.

"Back," I say.

The news of 1983 is speculative and slippery but the librarian secures this article with its explosive headline into the frame. She offers me her chair.

It's a long article. Too long. Too *po-angliyski.* My mother has always pushed me to learn English and I did, thinking it was professionally prudent to be able to speak it. But never did I expect to be so devastatingly, personally affected by not mastering the nuances of the language. Because I can understand the words before me, but they don't make understandable sentences. As for the conclusion—the thing that the not fully understood sentences must decide—there doesn't seem to be one. I can't read between the lines to find the source of skepticism. I can only put my index finger on a screen that keeps the reality of smudged newsprint and Soviet disinformation in the past: reports that Svetlana Dukovskaya had not made a public appearance in six months, not even as part of the Bolshoi's delegation to the state funeral of Party Secretary Leonid Brezhnev. Evidence of the removal of her portrait from the theater's hallways, the expulsion of her daughter from the Academy. Suggestions of a sudden decline of the internationally renowned ballerina's favor with officials.

I lose the thread. The words blur: *Officially sanctioned rumored alcoholic mentally disturbed unrequited spurned disfavor dangerous elements foreign adventures treachery espionage wreckage.*

I stop reading. I study the picture of my grandmother, Svetlana Dukovskaya. It shows her in her "signature role" of Coppelia.

Coppelia: a puppet, a decoy. Not much better than a doomed sacrificial maiden, when you come to think of it.

I pick up the magazines. These were published fifteen years later, when Svetlana would have been fifteen years older. Or, it would seem, dead. I quickly leaf through each one. Between them, there are fewer than 400 words spilled for my grandmother. Twenty-five of them are: *her death confirmed by Georgi Levshik, a close friend of the family, who has also announced an endowment in her name for the Bolshoi Ballet.*

"*Chort,*" I mutter. I'll be damned.

NINE
OPENING NIGHT

I watch the Bolshoi's opening night from stage left. I sit in the director's chair. The one that should have been filled by Pavel Vartukh.

"Dodging traffic," cracked Yuri, tonight's Prince, to the amusement of the guys' dressing room.

"Flu, I heard," said Olga with a shrug.

"Maybe you should go check on him, Lana. He might need some TLC?" That, of course, was Irina with a smirk.

The Met stagehand said he hadn't seen our artistic director, either. "But the lady, the Arkhipova lady, she's definitely in charge. She's the boss. Just wiggle over here to the left, would ya? Don't block the scene truck."

Anna, when I found her, just waved me away, as though it were a perfectly normal event for the artistic director to miss opening night of a New York tour.

"I think you've done enough already to cause tension,

Lana," she muttered tersely, eyes glued to her phone. "I'd thank you to keep quiet for the duration of the performance."

Shut up and carry on.

So here I am. Only half present. Cognizant of Tchaikovsky. Hunted by Stravinsky. Haunted also by the speculations of thirty years ago, preserved on flimsy film next door. If Marina had really been expelled from the Academy, if her mother had truly been crazy, or an alcoholic, or a spy . . . What does that say about the Dukovskaya legacy? What does it say about the reality now? That the Bolshoi forgives? The Bolshoi forgets? No. I don't think so.

The Sleeping Beauty is a big hit, though Irina's Aurora strikes me as a bit wobbly. The orchestra starts a bit below tempo, but adjusts quickly. The corps is in better form than usual. Yuri, stifling a sneeze during the bows, steps on Galya's toe. By 9:15, it is all over.

NINA IS WIRED AFTERWARD, chattering a mile a minute about the size of the stage and the stagehands. One of them, a handsome black guy with dyed hair, had serenaded her, she says.

"Khold me closer, tiny daaancer," she warbles, trilling every *r-r-r*. "Lana, you simply have to get out on that stage. It's marvelous."

I believe her. There's only so much you can see from backstage, but I felt the vibe that has so thrilled Nina. This is the Bolshoi, plus. This is platinum. This is the why. I'm happy for her. And yes, I want it, too. But not as much as I want to understand why the tombstone in Novodevichy cemetery has only one date on it. Not as much as I want to speak with my mother. Not as much as I want to bolt and find my own stage.

I check my phone once more. There is one text message, and I jump on it. It's from Stas: Tell your mother to stick to the truth. No stories.

An explosion of laughter all around me. Kiril has the Lilac Fairy tutu on his head and is prancing down the hall.

I text back: ??? Has something happened?

There is no answer.

I wait three minutes and then scoop up my things.

"Listen, Nina. Can I meet you back at the hotel? I need to call home."

Her face, all delight, transforms. It says, *Oh, I almost forgot.*

"Of course. Everything all right?"

I kiss her on the cheek and hurry past half-dressed fairies and cavaliers. I leap over a three-foot-long hillock of princess skirts and a phalanx of heraldic banners. I'm ten feet from the exit and I can already feel the relief of fresh air, of evening, of the street's inviting headlights—

Of Roma, waiting just up the block.

I push the doors open with both arms. I'm a battering ram. I'm dynamite. Where is this energy coming from? Is it because I believe I've got allies? No. I've got clues. I've got dreams so real.

"*Dobriy vecher,* Lana."

It's not his voice. Not Roma.

"Good evening, Georgi Levshik," I say.

He is leaning up against a showman's car, dressed in black tie. He's smaller than he appeared in the restaurant. But just as much the master of his castle. He extends a bouquet.

"I'm afraid I missed the performance. Unexpected business. It couldn't be helped. I'm sure you were a triumph."

"Oh, yes. A triumph in Converse."

He chuckles. "And at the beginning of a phenomenal career. If you will permit me, I will take those Converse and bronze them, Lana. To remind me of where it all began."

I realize he hasn't understood. He actually thinks I have just come from the stage, probably giddy with euphoria. Even more pathetic—he thinks it is his triumph as well. He is putting the flowers into my arms, perhaps expecting that I will thank him. And I can't restrain myself. I have to burst his stupid inflated bubble.

"I don't take flowers I haven't earned."

"Oh, don't be so proletarian, Lana. You danced. That's your job. That's all you need to do."

"No. No, I didn't. I did not dance tonight. What's more, I won't dance tomorrow."

His face hardens. "I was under the impression you were given a solo."

"What gave you that impression, Georgi?" I say, giving him the benefit of a first-name basis, but nothing more.

"Pavel Vartukh gave me that impression," he says.

I knew it. Proof of Vartukh's words: *You have a patron.*

"Pavel Vartukh is a washed-up, passed-out has-been," I spit at this flaccid old man. "You've been doing business with the wrong asshole. He didn't even make it to the theater tonight. He missed his own premiere."

Georgi reaches into his jacket. For a hysterical moment I imagine he's going to pull out a gun and force me back up on the stage. But it's just a phone. He punches a key and speaks into it: "*Nemedlenno.* Get over here now." He tucks the phone back into his jacket and says to me, "I'm going to clear all this up, Lana. Don't worry."

It's the last straw. I hurl the flowers in the gutter. I'm making a scene. I'm making a stand.

"There is only one thing I want from you, Dyadya Gosha," I say, dripping the *dyadya* like mud. "There's just one thing I want to know: *Chto sluchilos' s Svetlanoy?*"

HERE'S A BRIEF LANGUAGE lesson from a girl who speaks plainly: Linguists will tell you that the key to a culture rests in its language. You know . . . how the Inuit have, like, 200 ways to say "snow," and Africans have as many words for "relatives"; while Amazon jungle tribes probably have a dozen expressions for, I don't know, "snake venom."

Well, Russians invest all their nuances in variations of "death."

There are a dozen ways to ask what I'm asking: How did my grandmother die? *Kak ona umerla? Kak ona pogibla? Kak ona pokonchila soboy? Kak ubili?* How is it that my grandmother's dead? How did she end? How was she ended? How did she end herself? But there's only one way ask for the truth: What happened to Svetlana?

"*Chto sluchilos' s Svetlanoy?*" I ask again.

Georgi leans back against the car. A long black town car with tinted windows. I see the shadows of two men inside. A driver and a bodyguard. Neither look like Roma. He leans over to retrieve the flowers, the props of my defiance. Then he speaks: "Your mother couldn't stand not knowing the answer to that same question. That's why she left New York. She told me she had to find out: *Chto sluchilos' s Svetlanoy?* What became of Svetlana?"

He plucks at the rescued flowers. Petals fall to the ground. He's ratcheting the tension. Maybe he wants me to plead with him. I don't.

"I'll tell you the truth," he says, his voice hard. "I no longer care what happened to Sveta. I only care about what happens to Marina. Sveta disappeared into the KGB's files. I could have lost your mother just as easily. Don't think I didn't panic when she decided to return to Moscow."

"And in the end you lost her, anyway, didn't you?" I say.

He winces. "You spoke with her? Your mother?"

"To hell with my mother. She won't even answer my calls."

His hand is on my forearm again like a snake. I'm the small blind animal, once again. "What do you mean?" he says.

I twist my arm free with fury. "I mean just that. I haven't spoken to her since I left Moscow. She's MIA—"

The roar of Roma's motorcycle cuts me off. And now we are three.

Georgi to Roma: "No fucking around. This is urgent."

Georgi to me: "I'm going to show you my real bona fides. This. This I can fix."

It dawns on me suddenly, like a spasm: My mother has not lost her phone. She is not giving me the silent treatment. She is not too busy to call. Marina is missing. My mother has disappeared. My grandmother and my mother . . .

"I won't impose upon you again, Lana," Georgi Levshik says. "But I will not abandon your mother. Okay? Do you understand?"

I hear my stunned voice.

"Yes, Georgi . . . *Da, Dyadya Gosha*. Okay."

He drops my hands, cracks three knuckles in quick succession and climbs into his car.

"I will make this right," he says once more. And then he's gone.

THIS TIME THERE IS no overture. I take the helmet wordlessly and climb onto Roma's motorcycle. He turns south, and when Lincoln Center's gold fades from his mirror I am back in terra incognita. I wonder, briefly, if we have a destination. I don't care. There is nowhere for me to go.

We swim through the neon of Times Square. So many lights it is impossible to tell up from down. But my mood is dark as the deep sea. When you are submerged, there is no telling the top from the bottom. The ubiquity of light, I think, is no different from its utter absence.

But this is Manhattan and, it turns out, a landscape of all shades of light. South of Times Square the storefronts dim and the crowds thin. The sky is tiered in a procession of purples and we're headed into warm violet. Less pomp, more pizzazz. I'm vaguely aware that I am getting my own cinematic tour of New York by night. But it's like a silent movie. I can write my own script. Or I can play deaf. I feel the vibrations of this foreign place speak through the metal of Roma's motorcycle, up through the thin soles of my Converse. Like an ancient pagan, I'm soft-shoed. I have no armor. No boots and no bouquets. I'm naked.

When Roma stops the bike we are on a crowded, narrow street.

I pull off the helmet and hear laughter and music. It's live music, live laughter. Intimate and unrehearsed. There is nothing grand about this corner. No fountains, no banners. Just the intersection of nightlife and of New Yorkers at home.

"This is the Village," says Roma. "Are you hungry?"

"Not in the slightest."

"You need to eat."

How would he know? He stows the helmets and locks the bike. Then he takes my hand and we cross the street. We duck into a small pizzeria and the smell makes a liar out of me. I inhale the first slice. He buys another. We eat silently, standing at the window looking out into this place he calls "the Village."

"Which village is this?" I ask eventually. Food has helped.

"Greenwich Village," he says. "The West Village. The Village Vanguard Village."

"Vanguard," I say. "Sounds sort of revolutionary. Is this where the old Communists hang out?"

He smiles. "This is where the jazzmen hang out. The Village Vanguard is the most famous jazz club in New York. It's right next door."

"Oh, well. This makes sense. For me to be hanging out in jazz clubs and eating pizza instead of . . ." I don't finish my thought. After all, there is no instead of. I am only symbolically on tour. I am Bolshoi flotsam. Just ask Roma—I'm not here to dance. I'm here to "discover something." And what have I discovered? That Dukovskayas disappear.

As if reading my thoughts, he says: "Did you do it? Did you find anything?"

"Yes. Your boss bought his patronage with money in my grandmother's name. He was a friend of my family and a friend of the Bolshoi. It looks like only one friendship has lasted."

"Some friendships are one sided," says Roma. "Some friendships lie dormant."

"Where has he gone?" I ask.

"I really don't know."

I can't decide if this is the right answer. Roma is all potential. I want him innocent, even if that means ignorant. But I also want him to *know*, so he can tell me. I want it both ways. Mostly, I want to know that Georgi is, as he promised, *fixing this*. So I ask.

"Yes. I have to believe he is." Roma's voice is low.

"When he says he will do something, he does it. And
when he doesn't tell me where he is going, it's best that
I don't know."

I consider this: *Is this a good answer?*

"Is he as powerful as he says?"

"Absolutely."

"And he will make sure that my mother isn't . . . ?"
I can't say it. Because I don't know what it is that my
mother isn't, wouldn't, shouldn't.

"He will," Roma assures me.

"And he will do that, why?"

"Because he is devoted to her."

The door opens and a clutch of laughing teenagers enter the pizzeria. We watch them take their time
picking their slices; the whole thing is a game. Like the
dancers on the street earlier today, they are familiar to
me, but foreign. What is the word? *Carefree.*

"I've known that about Gosha for as long as I've
known him," Roma continues. "That's why I expected
him to be . . ." He pauses, rubs his chin. "I expected him
to be kinder to you. But then, I guess I also expected
you to be easier to be kind to."

I look at him sharply. "What does that mean? And
what's with these expectations? Why did you have any
expectations?"

"I mean that Gosha didn't know you. He still doesn't.
He just knew that Marina's daughter was coming and
that it was his chance."

"Chance for what?" My fists are clenched.

"To meet you," he says. Roma has ditched his paper

plate now, his eyes focused on mine, his face solemn. "To get to know you. Honestly, I think that's all he wanted."

My head is spinning. *What else might he have wanted? What is this strange American boy trying to talk me away from?*

"But I think maybe I know you better than he does at this point," Roma adds.

"Why. Because you saw me dance?" It comes out harsher than I mean it. Maybe because I hope it is true.

He clears his throat. He's spinning the glass jar of red pepper, it wobbles on its axis. He doesn't answer my question.

"In the library," Roma murmurs. "Did you look up Benjamin Frame?"

I grab the jar from his hands. "I did. He's a musician. Wrote about Stravinsky."

"He's a fantastic jazz pianist, too," he says.

"Let me guess. He's playing at the Village Vanguard."

"He is."

"Listen, Roma," I say, righting the pepper jar. "I thank you for your solicitousness. For making sure I eat. For knowing me well enough to get me the hell away from Lincoln Center for an hour. Really. Thanks. But I'm just not in the mood to listen to a bunch of intellectual grooviness. Not even some fantastic jazz pianist."

I ball up my napkin and aim it at the trash can. I'll sink it. Full stop. No argument. But it hits the rim.

Roma has the rebound.

"Lana, he's your father."

TEN
VANGUARD

The guy at the door of the Village Vanguard says the set is almost over.

"That's cool," says Roma.

The guy at the door says we still have to pay the cover.

"That's cool, too," says Roma, pulling out a wad of cash.

The guy at the door says we need to be twenty-one to enter.

"Tell Marcel to come out," says Roma.

Marcel is a skinny man with a long, grey ponytail and leather pants. He gives Roma a fake right hook to the jaw.

"Where you been, man?" he says. Then he tells Roma to put his damn money away and stop showing off in front of his girlfriend. He tells the guy at the door that Roma is on the always-welcome list. Then he tells me to enjoy the show, what's left of it.

I throw a glance at Roma. "What?" he asks, avoiding my eyes. "I'm a well-rounded music lover."

Inside, all the tables are full. Roma and I take two stools at the bar. There are five or maybe six musicians, playing the sort of cool, nonchalant music that only Americans play. The piano is pushed into the corner out of the lights. His, the pianist's, is the only face I can't see.

I turn my back to the stage and focus on the raised round rim of the bar. I am clutching it.

"Are you sure you want to do this?" Roma asks. "We can come back another time. You can call him. You can . . ."

"Shhh. I want to hear him play."

The next five minutes are endless. An endless chord progression that keeps promising to end but doesn't. And then it does. The crowd hoots. The snare shivers, a wire brush on my spine. I grab Roma's wrist and he bends to confer, but I just want his watch. It is 10:42.

I rise from the bar and walk to the stage area to meet my father, Benjamin Frame. B., I think. I'm walking blindly into an eddy of musicians, fans, friends. People he knows, people he's comfortable with. People he recognizes. I wait, my heart racing, my mind blank. A big guy, the bass player, takes a step to the right. I see him. There is no question. I push forward. I am standing by the piano in the Village Vanguard looking at a man with my nose, my high cheekbones, and my hand in his.

I see the start of recognition on Benjamin Frame's face, but I tell him anyway—in Russian.

He responds in Russian: "I'm sorry, say that again . . ."

"Lana. My name is Lana Dukovskaya."

He sits down hard on the piano bench. My hand still in his.

"Jesus," he says.

My father shows his surprise in English.

He opens his mouth, but nothing comes out.

I am memorizing him as he struggles. The straight hairline beneath dark curls. The thoughtfulness of his creased brow. The grey at his temples. The sinews of his forearms, soft in the dimmed lights. The unpressed shirt, misbuttoned but becoming. The way he has wrapped his fingers in mine so that I can't let go.

He tries again. "I'm sorry. I'm . . . I'm shocked. It's wonderful. A shock. A wonder-shock."

I tuck away another observation about my father: his Russian is no longer native, and my presence is foreign. I'm momentarily angry. He is the one on home territory. This should not be harder for him than for me.

Someone bumps into me and says in English, "Ben! I've got this great recording . . ."

Benjamin Frame stands and pulls me to his side, swatting away smiles like mosquitoes. He doesn't let go of me until we are in a booth in the corner of the club, hidden from the crowd. Sitting across the table from him, I am struck mute.

"I don't know where to start," he says.

"Would you like me to?" I ask.

"That seems unfair."

"I'm used to unfair."

"How did . . . how did you get here?"

I see Roma watching from the end of the bar. I nod to him. *I'm okay.*

Benjamin Frame follows my gaze.

"He brought me," I explain. "That boy told me. I didn't know about you until tonight. But he told me." I feel tears threatening to tell the rest of the story. I barrel on. "My mother never told me. No one ever told me. I'm not sure why . . . why it had to be Roma."

"Roma . . ." repeats Benjamin. He's searching the bar, looking for a better answer. "He brought you from . . ."

"From Lincoln Center."

He leans back. I see something battle his confusion and win. He is proud. He is pleased.

"Of course," he says. "You are with the Bolshoi. Of course you are."

I feel his eyes on me, scrutinizing me for signs of my mother. It's pointless. My features are his.

"How old are you, Lana?"

"Eighteen, just."

"Can I ask you something?"

"May 7, 1995," I answer before he can ask. And then I ask him: "Are you really my father?"

He takes a deep breath and works his hand through his hair. I mimic the motion.

"I think, yes, that it is very possible. Likely even. The last time I saw your mother was . . . yes, I think so."

He looks at me and focuses. His eyes are dark and warm.

"Is she in New York?"

I shake my head. I don't tell him that I don't, in fact, know where she is. "She is not in New York," I offer.

"Please tell me about her," he says.

"If you don't mind, I'd rather you did."

"What do you mean?"

"I mean, please tell me about my mother. She's the goddamn sphinx."

He swallows, fidgets in the booth. To his credit, he doesn't look around, though I can feel a few eyes on us. "What do you know, Lana?"

So very little, I think. But I say: "I know that she came here when she was seventeen. With her father. Without her mother. I know her father died while they were here. I know she studied dance at Juilliard and moved back to Moscow after the Soviet Union collapsed. I know she joined the Bolshoi but quit after a few years. When she got pregnant, I think."

He's looking at me and nodding. But not a nod, like: *You're right.* A nod, like: *Go on.* "You don't know anything more about Viktor, your grandfather?" he asks. "Or about Svetlana?"

I shake my head, though hearing him say her name makes my heart trip. "Svetlana was a ballerina. She danced the Chosen One. That's it. That's all." I reconsider. "And also, I guess, she's dead."

"And Viktor?"

"Killed in a nightclub in Brooklyn. I don't know when. I'm guessing Georgi Levshik was Ma's guardian after that. Until she left."

Benjamin Frame leans forward with his elbows on the table.

"That's . . ." He's searching for the word. "That's just a skeleton of the story."

I nod. I lean forward. My hands are a fist. My knuckles touch his. He takes a deep breath. He closes his eyes.

"Please tell me." I say.

"The first woman I ever fell in love with was your mother. It was in Brooklyn. It was New Year's Eve. She wore a sapphire-blue dress with her shoulders bare. The next time she wore that dress was at City Hall. She married me in that dress. We insisted on it. The marriage. If Marina was going back to Russia, she was going to go back as an American citizen. We wanted to make sure she didn't close the door behind her."

"We?" I ask.

"Me. My parents. And Georgi. Georgi agreed. Georgi, maybe, most of all." He looks at me. He takes my hands without leaving my eyes. It's incredibly odd, to see yourself in a stranger. "Of course, she never came back. Only I did."

"So it was just a business arrangement? Your marriage."

"The marriage, yes. Us: no." His eyes meet mine again. "No."

There's a squawk from the sound system. The jukebox takes over. Benjamin Frame drops my hand and gestures to the barman. *Turn that down.* The music recedes.

Vot, he says. "And so . . . and so I've had to rethink

a lot of things over the years. Reassess what happened. What I thought would happen. What I hoped would happen. And many things are less clear to me now than they were at the time. But I've never doubted that. That she and I—Marina and I—we were in love. Your mother, I believe, loved me. Once."

The thing that crosses his face can only be pain.

"Why did she leave?" I ask.

"Why did she leave? Well, she left America because she was sure that her mother was still alive and that she could find her. She left me . . . I guess for the same reason."

I lean back in the booth cushions. "I don't get it. What did you have to do with her mother?"

"I doubted."

"You doubted."

"I doubted that we would find her. But I also doubted Marina and what she believed about herself and her mother. You see, Svetlana had information. Or she said she did. She claimed she had something like second sight, prescience. She had visions. She said she knew a secret that the state didn't want told and she threatened to tell."

"About the Bolshoi?" I ask.

He shakes his head. "No. Marina thought it was much bigger than that. Something about biological weapons. Something about civilian deaths and a botched cover-up of a biological contamination at the laboratory where your father worked, Lukino. She must have shared her concerns with someone other than your grandfather. She whispered too loudly. She disappeared into the secret police's 'psychiatric rehabilitation centers.' That's where they put her when she gave voice to her visions. That's why Marina and Viktor had to defect when they did. They would have gone into the prison camps, too."

I exhale loudly. It's a lot. It's everything I imagined plus some crazy psychic shit. It's what Marina wrote. *I once had a dream that I would see my mother again . . .*

"My mother—did she have them too? Visions?"

"Yes. I guess that's what they were. She believed they were."

"You didn't?"

His answer does not come as quickly as the one about Svetlana. He won't admit that he doubted.

"She had foreseen her father's death, that's true enough," he says. "I was there when she did. And she was certain that she had also seen her mother alive. I figured it was what we would now call post-traumatic stress disorder. In fact, with the passage of time and her acceptance of her life here . . . the spells, visions, whatever they were, pretty much stopped. But then the wall fell. The Soviet Union collapsed. She was free to go back and she was determined. Svetlana loomed large again. Of course I went with her. I had promised. We were married. And then I made a terrible mistake. I doubted."

"That Svetlana was alive?" I press.

He shrugs. "I began to look into the KGB files. I found evidence about Lukino, but nothing about Svetlana. The trail went cold. Honestly, it had never been hot. She was arrested on November 10, 1983. She was institutionalized on November 15, 1983, and that was the end. The ward where she was originally held moved its patients out in the late 1980s; the records were destroyed or lost during the confusion of the next decade. There was nothing more."

I study him—his gaze now on something far from this bar, this Village. Benjamin Frame is a million miles away when he slips into the present tense: "*Eto vsyo.* That's all."

I give him a moment to come back. Then I say that I know how unreasonable my mother can be. How stubborn: "But to hold you responsible for what happened to her mother . . . that's not fair," I conclude.

He shifts again, slightly. He tugs his ear. "No," he agrees. "But there were other things. Things more . . . more tangible than Svetlana."

I can almost feel him wringing his hands under the table.

"I maybe could have kept searching. I could have hit the road, visited all the dead ends of the old Gulag prison system. But I decided that the search was not good for Marina's emotional health. And it just became untenable. She decided I was keeping the truth from her, protecting her somehow. When in fact, there was nothing I could hide. There was nothing at all."

"So how did it end?"

Again, the evasive shrug. "She asked me to leave in November 1994. It was the eleventh anniversary of her mother's disappearance. I begged her to put it behind her. Instead, she put me behind her."

I watch him choose these words. I imagine Marina

taking a huge leap, one that this man—even with his long piano fingers—couldn't catch. I am sure it is the last time she acted with such resolve.

"Do you think of her?" I ask.

"All the time."

"But you didn't know," I say. I'm not sure if I mean about me, or about Marina's discarded dreams and lonely life.

"I didn't. Of course not."

We are silent for a minute. The bar hums on without us.

"And it's dawning very slowly on me, I'm afraid," he continues. His voice is shaky. "How bittersweet it is to know that I left something. That we have something, still, to show for how hard we tried."

Me. He means me. I am "bittersweet."

"I'm so very, very sorry, Lana. That I have missed all this time."

It is the truth and I feel it wash over me like a baptism. I have been, I think, underwater. It's on the tip of my tongue to tell him that it's not his fault. That we have time now. That I will stay in this booth and make this Village our Vanguard until we can be reunited—my mother, my father, and me.

But I'm cut off by the most conflicted signal I could ask for—it's my phone ringing for the first time in three days. But it's not my mother. The caller ID is Nina's. And when I answer, I am only able to understand between hysterics that "the shit is going down."

ELEVEN
REVERSAL OF FORTUNE

Roma makes good time back uptown. He didn't want to. He wanted me to stay with Benjamin Frame. "I'll feel better if you keep your distance from all that," he pleaded outside the club. "At least until Gosha resurfaces."

I literally had to put my hands over my ears. It was a siren's call. Of course I wanted to stay there, too. I'd just found him. Just. But it was already maybe too much.

"It's a bad idea. I can't ask for more trouble tonight. Nina needs me. Benjamin Frame definitely doesn't."

"What do you mean? It looked like it was going well," Roma whispered with a glance at the door, my father behind it somewhere.

"It is. And I want it to stay that way. I don't want him to know that Marina's gone AWOL and that I've gone rogue. That will only make him wish I had never walked in here with more Bolshoi baggage."

It was the phrase that Nina had used. *Gone rogue.* Her voice was anxious and her message garbled. But it was clear that she was bearing the brunt of my absence: "That's what she said, Lana. Anna Dmitrievna is telling everyone you've gone rogue, and that you've poisoned Vartukh against us and that I should tell the other girls that you have been threatening me or otherwise she'll accuse me of colluding with rogue elements."

I'd made my apologies to Benjamin, my father. Of course he understood very well that I needed to get back and rest up for tomorrow's performance.

"I'll be there," he'd promised.

It was an awkward goodbye. The strange exchange of numbers. Him leaning over to look at my screen. "No. three-six-five not three-five-six. Yes. Great. Well. I sure look forward to . . . and thank you—Roma, you said your name is? Roma. Thank you. Okay. We'll talk, right Lana? We'll talk soon. Tomorrow, yes?"

We are all the way back at the hotel, climbing off the bike, before it occurs to me to ask Roma the very obvious question.

"How did you know how to find him—my father?"

"I asked," Roma replies.

"You asked."

"Yes. I asked Gosha. He told me."

"When?"

"Like I said. I've known about you, Lana, for some time. It was probably close to a year ago that Gosha told me the Bolshoi would be coming, and that he hoped you would, too. He had never shown an interest in such a young dancer. So I asked. He told me everything."

"Everything."

Roma is unapologetic. "Yes. Yes, I think so."

"Did he tell you why my mother won't speak to him?"

"Yes, he did."

His frankness is disarming. I hand him the helmet, though something makes me want to keep it.

"And why is that?" I ask. "Why won't my mother speak to him?"

He glances at the entrance to the hotel. "We have time for all your questions. Gosha is a good man, Lana. He's good to the people he cares about. I can help you understand how to ask and be answered. Obviously, whatever I know is just . . . well, just what I know. I don't know you. I said I did. But . . ." His voice softens. "Three days ago I thought I'd be babysitting a bubble-headed ballerina who would sit quietly with her newfound Dyadya Gosha and clap her hands with delight. I never expected . . ." He shakes his head and pivots away from me. "I don't know you. But I want to. And that takes more than explaining. That takes listening."

And to think that last night he was just my lift across town.

I take one step closer to him.

He's a solid foot taller than me. I lean my head against his chest. I want to ask him if he is really this kind. But I don't.

"I need to straighten out this bullshit with Arkhipova," I say. "We can talk tomorrow."

He puts one hand on top of my head, musses it in a way that tells me he gives a mighty scalp massage. "I'll be here at sunrise," he says.

"I'm guessing that means you'll be here all night."

Roma lifts a teasing eyebrow. "Don't get cocky, you. You won't tell me your life story tonight, and I've got places to be."

I watch him speed off.

"LANA, COULD YOU TELL us where you have been?"

Anna Arkhipova is sitting in a leather chair in the lobby, stirring a cup of tea. Apparently, she is not the only one who wants to know. She has brought Nina, Tatiana, and Olga to witness my dressing-down. She has also brought two stone-faced men: Vlad, her bodyguard, and a nameless backup.

Nina sits with her eyes cast down. Olga is filing her nails.

"Lana?" Anna taps a foot. It's almost funny, her classic impatience.

"At the Village Vanguard," I say. "I caught the last set."

"And do you know what has transpired in your absence?" she asks archly. I can't tell if she is enjoying her cruelty or just administering it, like a prescribed dose of medicine.

"Your mother has been arrested," she says.

As if on cue, everyone in the room who had been watching me looks away. And everyone who had not been looking at me does now. All except Nina. She is still studying the floor. Her cheeks flush red. My cockiness vanishes. Because

I know it's true. It explains Marina's silence. Explains the messages from Stas. Explains my sudden need for Georgi to be Gosha. Explains my about-face from revulsion to trust. *Da, Dyadya Gosha, please fix this.*

"That's right," says Anna. "The man they detained last week has been interrogated. It turns out he wasn't some sociopath nut job after all."

She takes a sip from her cup. It rattles slightly in its saucer when she puts it back down.

"He looked the part—another aggrieved lunkhead with extremist views, a chip on his shoulder and debts to pay—but that's not what he was. Not exactly. I mean, maybe he had debts. Certainly, he needed money." She looks up at me. Her eyes are steady but her upper lip twitches, like she can hardly control her amusement. "He was a hit man, Lana. And he says your mother hired him."

My eyes are steady, too. "That's absurd and you know it," I reply.

"How so?" she asks with fake interest, as if I've just told her that she reminds me of a famous film star.

"My mother has no money. She has no motive."

Anna Arkhipova nods. "But she has a daughter who does. A daughter who inherited great talent from her mother . . . and who knows what else? Maybe her lack of restraint."

I feel like I will throw up if I answer her.

"They brought her in last night," my mother's old friend continues. She places her empty cup down on the saucer and stands. "She's in Butyrskaya prison awaiting charges. We've done our best to keep the information from the press until we can fashion a response. I'm afraid we'll have to do the same with you."

I should bolt right now, of course. But I don't.

"I see that you've not seen any reason to keep this information from the company," I say, gesturing to the other girls. "Are they to help fashion a response? Or are you going to leave that to Pavel, who's been spewing drunken nonsense all day?"

Tatiana inhales sharply.

Shit. That was a false step.

"Actually, Lana," Arkhipova hisses, stepping close, "we had hoped to keep his condition under wraps as well. As should you, given that you were the last one to enjoy his company." I can feel her breath on my face. Peppermint tea. "What on earth did you let that poor man drink?"

Olga is watching me. Tatiana is watching me. Vlad and the other guy are stone-faced. Nina speaks up, barely. "Anna Dmitrievna, Lana was with me this morning."

"Yes, Nina, you told me," Anna snaps back. "She was with you discussing the origins of a certain variation, which she thought Pavel might help clarify. As if he didn't have plenty of other things to worry about on opening night."

Nina's eyes dart from me to Anna, and then into a hole to hide.

You stupid, dear girl, I think.

"Is that why they are all down here?" I demand. "To report on how I've been spending my time, now that I've been dragged to New York for nothing?"

"Well, it couldn't be helped," says Anna airily. "There's a leak in your room."

A leak. She makes it sound ambiguous. Maybe not the radiator or the showerhead. Maybe a mole. Or a rat. "The girls are just waiting a room reassignment. And you, Lana, will be staying with me where I can keep a close eye on you."

It's only now that I notice: our bags are packed and assembled by the front desk. *Reassignment.* I tamp down nausea. I calculate the time in Moscow once more. What do they serve for breakfast in Butyrskaya's central holding? "You can't possibly believe this," I say again. "I want to speak with Vartukh."

"He's quite indisposed," she says. "And anyway, what can he do?"

"What can he do? What can the artistic director of the ballet do?" I shout. "He can admit that he and he alone is to blame for Daniela's ruined career. She's the only innocent victim here. Because she was in the wrong place at the wrong time, and on the wrong arm."

I catch my breath in the silence.

Anna sniffs. "What exactly are you insinuating, Lana? Are you accusing your friend of inappropriate relations with her director?"

My God. She's done it again. She's turned my words on themselves. All my indignation has been reduced to cattiness.

"It wouldn't be the first time, Anna Dmitrievna. Just the first time it ended so badly."

She shakes her head. I want to snap it off her neck.

"Lana, Lana. You are, of course, right. There are always girls who are dissatisfied with their station. Girls who give up on the hard work and patience that the corps demands. Girls who drive their directors to drink and find a benevolent uncle to push them out on the stage. Girls who believe they are owed some sort of legacy."

I feel the heat rise to my face. I feel my disbelief overwhelm me. I don't know who she is accusing—Marina? Or me?

"Ninochka," says Anna, her eyes not leaving mine. "Hand us the letter, dear."

Nina's hand is trembling as she holds out the yellowed paper covered in my mother's inky blue hand. Anna takes it and reads her own carefully crafted summary: *"Danilov has hinted I will move out of the corps by spring. You will have to come for that, Gosha—no excuses! I've made my decision. I want this more than I want love."*

My knees finally give out. My everything gives out.

HOW I SLEPT THAT night, I don't know. After my scene in the lobby it was all just a hellish blur. The bodyguard, Vlad, stepped forward and took my elbow. The other prick leapt to help and together they lifted me across the lobby.

Anna followed, yammering in English at the surprised hotel desk clerk about stage fright and nerves. I was begging Nina to *tell them, please*. But Nina had apparently already told. And what I wanted her to tell, she had no one to tell to. She knew nothing about Dyadya Gosha. Nothing about Roma. I heard her sobbing as the elevator closed.

In Anna's suite, I fell silent. She played the role of a mother whose spoiled child has just recovered from an embarrassing temper tantrum.

"I'm sure it will be better in the morning. Things always are."

She got on the phone with the front desk and requested that the girls downstairs be put in single rooms. "On separate floors, be a dear," is the last thing I heard before I fell sound asleep.

WHEN I AWAKE IT is almost noon.

I am alone. My bag is in the corner next to me. On top of it, Gosha's envelope lies prominently. My dance bag, too, is here. And a silver tray set with breakfast. What is not here is Arkhipova. Or my phone. I ransack the suite but it is nowhere to be found. I pick up the hotel phone, but there's no dial tone. I scream in frustration.

Heavy footsteps from the small vestibule: it's the prick, Arkhipova's second bodyguard, with his hand inside his jacket. I tell him not to shoot.

Clearly, he's too stupid even to joke around.

"I just want my phone," I say.

He shrugs and disappears back into the alcove.

I eat breakfast. I take my time. I take a long bath, using all of the complimentary products.

When I am done I call to the prick. I don't really know him. I know Vlad. Vlad has been Arkhipova's body-guard for years. This one is new. He just showed up here in New York, for the tour. No one else in the theater has a bodyguard. Not the head of the box office; not Elena Krasnova, the prima who received death threats when she broke off her "sponsorship" with a well-known gangster; not even Vartukh, victim of a brazen public attempt on his life.

"Am I allowed to leave?" I ask.

He puts a knuckle against his nostril and snorts.

"Hay fever," he explains. "No."

"What's your name?" I ask.

"Ivan."

"Ivan, can you tell me, is there any news?"

His cheek twitches once. Something like sympathy. "The English princess had her baby," he says.

"Can I use your phone, Ivan?

"Nope."

"I won't call. I just want to get on the Internet," I explain. My mother might be in the headlines by now.

Ivan holds up his phone so I can see the screen.

"No Internet. Only Angry Birds."

I go back into the bedroom of Anna's royal suite. I check the windows for fire escapes and the bathroom for ballerina-size vents. I pick up the hotel phone receiver six times in a row. I turn on the television and curse twenty-five stations selling exercise equipment and gold coins. I sit on the bed and wonder why Nina is such a craven ninny. I wonder why I couldn't have gotten here faster last night and whether it would have made a difference. I wonder where Roma is and if he would hear me if I yell loud enough. I go back to the window. No air shaft—just all of Central Park stretching into the week-end. I look down, ten floors.

All of New York streaming toward the park. No one waiting on the street, waiting since sunrise.

I had wanted so much to believe him. To believe that there was business beneath Gosha's bluster. That he was going to fix this. That I would wake up this morning, chat with my mother—and, oh, brunch with Roma. Maybe skip the performance and take in some jazz. Idiot. And to think that I pitied Nina for what I mistook for stupidity.

I kick Anna's oversize wheeled bag in frustration. It pops open, spilling cosmetics and pill bottles. I pick up one with the label of a Moscow pharmacy. Anna Dmit-rievna, it appears, has trouble sleeping. I pick up a second bottle, red plastic—not the kind you get with a prescrip-tion, but the kind you probably buy in one of those health stores full of powders and supplements and steroids. DNPX reads the black label, APPETITE SUPPRESSOR. Anna also has trouble keeping her not-so-slim figure.

I rifle through the rest of Anna's belongings, cursing her name, Nina's name, and Pavel's name as I do. I find a personal stash of peppermint tea and too many pairs of Spanx. But nothing that will help to make this right. I'm a prisoner. My captor is a vain, vindictive woman who has decided to throw my mother under the bus. But why?

I look again at the sleeping pills. I wonder where Var-tukh is now. Drunk again? Passed out? Locked up in a regal suite somewhere on this floor? I didn't believe it yesterday. Today I do. He's lost control of the ballet. And I'm just as helpless. I laugh out loud. And to think that I came rushing back here for Nina. Poor, helpless Nina. Who will be warming up for her solo within the hour.

From the vestibule, I hear Ivan's phone ring. "*Da. Lana zdes*. She's here. *Seychas.*"

He enters the bedroom and hands me my jacket and my Converse.

"*Poshli*, let's go."

I pull on my shoes and grab my dance bag. Outside the suite, I scan the hallway, but there's nowhere to run.

Anna Arkhipova is waiting in the lobby, all heat and purpose, like a controlled blaze. She says: "Nina is nowhere to be found. There's forty minutes to curtain. Lana, you are the Chosen One."

TWELVE
THIRD TIME

The day that Nina went missing, I wanted her gone.
Not permanently maybe. But pretty much immediately. *She betrayed me*, I had thought. And when Anna
pronounced her gone, I said to myself: *she got what's
coming.*

Not that I knew what was coming, mind you.

Arkhipova pushed me into a waiting car and barked
orders into her phone. Costume. Program inserts. No
police. No press. I imagined Vartukh on the other end of
the phone. Why not? All our roles have been reversed.

When we arrived at the stage door, I looked up the
street. There was no one but the chicken man.

Arkhipova led me at a clip through a large room occupied by a row of vending machines and a single long
table where two harried young women were hunched
over a paper cutter. A pile of confetti and several boxes
of programs lay at their feet. One of the slips flew from

the cutter and landed on my arm. I recognized the crooked announcement of an eleventh-hour change in the program.

TONIGHT'S PERFORMANCE OF DANSE SACRALE
WILL BE PERFORMED BY LANA DUKOVSKAYA.

You might think that this would have triggered the obvious thought: *I am the substitute. First Daniela, then Nina . . . I'm next. I'm the sacrificial victim.* Instead, I thought of Svetlana. I thought of my mother and her jealous guardian instinct. Marina and her belief in Svetlana's legacy.

I stood motionless before the costume fitter. I decided not to think anymore. As she adjusted the soft suede sheath of the Chosen One to hang above my knee, I even forgot Nina.

Ten minutes was all they gave me to warm up. Then I was standing stage right, my hair blue black and shiny, and my feet on fire. I watched the curtain fall on *Les Sylphides* and the small hole in the corps that Nina's cohorts had artfully hidden. I stepped out into the live music of a possessed forest of stage lights and into *The Rite of Spring.*

I was the Chosen One. And I rejoiced.

I possessed the stage and spun it with defiance. I conducted the orchestra solo, turning my captors into a captive audience and stopping time for four minutes to celebrate the most ancient cycle of life. I was an athlete, a revelation. I was elevation and escalation. I was a human distress signal, spelling my SOS in anatomical letters. That was me—breathing heavily in thunderous applause, my fists brandished as the curtain fell.

That was me: a stooge, exulting in my fellow dancers' shocked reverence as I stepped off the stage. Me, accepting Anna Dmitrievna's praise and request that I sign this little girl's program: *Especially for you, Lana.* Me, following Arkhipova into the pressroom to meet my smitten critics.

Call me naïve, but when Nina disappeared, I thought we both had gotten what we deserved.

THAT WAS ONE MINUTE and a lifetime ago.

Now I am standing in the flash of cameras, my smile fading as I understand these are not the culture critics and the magazine photographers. These are the newshounds. Anna Arkhipova is telling these reporters that Nina has turned up, and in a bad way. "Toxicologists have not confirmed . . . recovery is uncertain. Absolutely not intentional. Ms. Oleynikova has no history of drug abuse or substance abuse of any kind . . . in fact, this turn of events is really highly . . . suspect."

The reporters with their microphones and notebooks fling questions in Russian and in English. I struggle to understand.

"Are you saying that it was not an overdose, but a poisoning?"

"I will not speculate further on the matter," Anna states. "I will only repeat that one of our junior dancers,

Nina Oleynikova, has been hospitalized after the consumption of a high dosage of an ultra-thermogenic anabolic steroid sometime in the last twelve hours."

Another reporter asks if Anna can confirm the whereabouts of Pavel Vartukh. She doesn't bat an eyelash.

She says, "Pavel Vartukh is recovering from a series of unfortunate events. The recent attempt on his life, combined with the pressures of the tour may be at the root of his current state of health. He has returned to Moscow for convalescence."

Now she turns to me. I see red. The red of her lipstick, her flushed chest, and all the flags waving backstage at Lincoln Center. From the journalists a single question: "Do you have any comment, Ms. Dukovskaya?"

I shake my head and back out of the room.

The reporter shouts, in Russian: "Please, Lana, any comment?"

Anna doesn't try to stop me from fleeing.

I HAVE NO PHONE. I have no phone and I am all alone. I was a triumph on stage less than a half hour ago, and now I'm on the street—anonymous, my costume hidden under blue jeans and my jacket. It's good that I brought my trench coat on tour to New York. I brought it because I thought it was becoming. I wasn't anticipating going on the lam in New York City.

I'm on the street, putting it all together.

Daniela attacked. And not by me. Vartukh drugged. And not by me. Nina poisoned. And not by me. And yet, I know this is all about me.

Shards of yesterday:

Man with bad fucking aim . . .

Pavel Vartukh gave me that impression . . .

God damn him. Georgi Levshik, my patron.

I hurl my dance bag at the wall that is on the south side of Lincoln Center Plaza. Anyone passing by would think I'm a disappointed dancer, just denied a lead role. But it's worse. Not denied. Deluded. I have been deluded. If I swing this bag hard enough, fast enough, over and over, I can forget that. I say it as I batter the walls with my only weapon: *he is the deluded one.*

Georgi Levshik is as deluded and sick as my mother. He can call it loyalty. He can call it love. I will call it an old man clinging to youth, to the relevance he once had and the power he never did. He thought he could put me on the stage and make things right for my mother? That I would be her proxy, just as soon as he cleared the obstacles? He didn't rush off last night to find my mother. He rushed off to fix Vartukh. And then he fixed Nina so that I would have the solo. And Daniela . . . how many young men on motorcycles do Levshik's bidding?

As if in answer—a sound too horrible for me to believe it was ever welcome—I hear the sound of Roma's Suzuki pulling up beside me.

There is a split second as my body recalibrates. If I run he would never catch me. That's how much adrenaline I have. But I don't run. I direct all my hysteria at his body. I am possessed, I am brutal, I am on top of him, inflicting damage. I think there is blood. I know there are shouts. There is also an undercurrent, fast, strong and deep, trying to absorb it all. It makes the sound *LanaLanaLanaLana*. I am still punching him when it changes to *stopstopstop*. I'm still yelling, accusing him, when the undercurrent pulls harder, sapping my strength.

He has me by both arms. My head is on his chest. There is a deep scratch down his neck. His helmet and his gloves are in the gutter ten feet away. There's a curious crowd around us.

"Tell them you're okay," he whispers. "Tell them you are okay, or you will have the police here. Are you ready for that? Are you ready to tell the police what has happened or will you please tell me first?"

I want to fight more, and I could; I have the strength. But it's hard to fight when you're crying. I never knew that before. I knew it was hard to dance when you're crying. Now I know it's the same.

"What's happened, Lana?" he breaths. "What's wrong?"

I pull away from him and ask, my voice a hoarse croak: "Where is she? What have they done to her?"

As I do, I see the onlookers continue on their way. A physical struggle is a spectacle. Words, shouted or not, reduce it to the ordinary. They disperse, with a few backward glances—just to make sure.

"She's safe," Roma says. "She's with Gosha. He kept his word, Lana. He's there now. As we speak. He went himself to release her."

I blink stupidly. Roma is talking about my mother. Gosha has gone to Moscow to release my mother from

Butyrskaya prison. He is fixing it, just as he promised. How confusing.

"Where's *Nina*?" I ask. This time a whisper.

"Nina?"

"Nina Oleynikova. A dancer. A sweet, simple, not spectacular dancer who was to perform her first solo today. But she didn't. I did."

Roma's face swims into focus. I don't recognize it. I've seen his face calm, disinterested, handsome as hell and, last night, tender. But I've never seen this. Alarm. He turns his back on me for just a moment and when he looks at me again, his hands are clasped in a symbol of prayer. "I beg you, Lana. Tell me she's not—"

"She's in a hospital somewhere, Roma, and I think Georgi Levshik is why."

"I can't believe . . . He wouldn't . . ."

"Wouldn't what? Wouldn't use his big-man status? Wouldn't do something despicable to get me onstage? Get himself back in good standing with my mother? Who, rightly it seems, told him good riddance a long time ago?"

He holds up a hand to explain. But I don't think he can. "I know what you are thinking. You are thinking that Gosha left just after last night's performance, when you told him that you would not be dancing . . ."

"Yes. And now both Vartukh and Nina are, to quote Arkhipova, 'convalescing.' So, yeah, that's exactly what I am thinking."

"Please, Lana. I can prove it." He unbuttons the breast pocket of his jacket and pulls out his phone. He scrolls quickly. I watch the blue light reflected in his eyes. He taps the screen and holds it up to me.

I'm looking at an e-ticket. It's for Georgi Levshik. The 7:50 A.M. flight out of JFK airport. Arriving in Moscow not long ago, just around the time I stepped out onto the stage of the Metropolitan Opera House, thinking of no one but myself.

"Georgi flew to Moscow this morning, Lana. He is not even here. He's not here. He didn't do it. The last ballerina he took to lunch was you, Lana. He's in Moscow. He went to get your mother released."

I consider this. I feel a shudder convulse me. "And you, Roma? Picked up any ballerinas on your bike since I left you?"

The shake of his head is too slow, too heavy. "I am on your side."

"Why should I believe you?"

"Because I haven't lied to you. Not ever."

"You've had little chance to," I remind him.

"I've told you the truth."

I cannot argue with that. He's the only one who has told me the truth.

"I'm going to my father," I say. I step out to flag a cab and then I stop and slump to the curb, back at defeat. "I don't know where he is. I don't have my phone. I have no idea where to find him."

"I'll take you," he says.

"No! No, you won't. Just tell me where he lives."

"Okay." He's like a bomb-defusing expert. Or someone locked in a cage with a tiger. Small movements, soothing voice, his eyes locked on me, as he reaches again for his phone. "Okay. Just let me find the address. I'll write it down."

A van pulls up behind us. A news van. And behind it is another. Two white vans with their letters rushing off the side panels, eager to break the story. It dawns on me that nobody in the pressroom asked me about the arrest of my mother. But now, I know they will. Gosha may be en route to Moscow, but the story hasn't waited for him. Anna Arkhipova has let it out.

A short man with a long microphone jumps from the first van. The Russian-language channel, RNR—Realniye Novosti Rossii.

"Lana! Lana Dukovskaya! *Skazhite pozhaluysta . . .* What can you tell us about . . . ?"

I rather suspect he might be able to tell me more than I can tell him. So I don't answer. I climb onto the seat of the Suzuki like the tiger that knows it's been beat. Roma doesn't need any encouragement. We screech away from the curb and cross Tenth Avenue against the light. Then we are hugging a corner and flying down the highway with its views of the Hudson River, whitecaps racing with us.

Roma is urgent, dodging the yellow cabs. There are no more red lights. There is nothing to tell my heart to stop. I'm pressed tight to his leathered back. I can taste salt on it.

We slip underground at the tip of Manhattan. Though we are there for less than a minute, when we emerge it feels like evening. Another river, another skyline across the water, and a sign for the Brooklyn Bridge.

I recognize the arches from postcards or textbooks. I might have identified it as the Tower of London: the sign that you have fallen from grace. Once you were a queen; now you are a prisoner. Roma downshifts, entering a rickety approach that winds itself serpentine onto the bridge. I feel light-headed as we slow in the miasma of car exhaust.

"Where are we going?" I shout, certain my voice can't survive.

But Roma hears me.

"Brooklyn," he says. And with whiplash, we are flying across the river into the distance.

ACT THREE
THE RITE OF SPRING
BROOKLYN

THIRTEEN
BRIGHTON BEACH

When Roma stops, I am lost. Brooklyn means nothing to me. It's where the grid ends. Where the long avenues quit and the sky retakes its advantage. It is where piers and barges and shipping containers hunker low under the flat purple skies. It is miles from Lincoln Center. It's where an evening storm gathers on the horizon.

I see every nation hurrying for home: Old women flying the tails of their bright-colored saris in the wind. Young women in long dark skirts pushing strollers laden with plastic bags bearing ancient alphabets. Larger clusters of boys, racing the traffic lights, trailing prayer curls and pious aprons. A tall man with a headdress of dreadlocks, dancing to music in his head.

When Roma stops, we are on a treelined boulevard surrounded by an old generation of Russians. On the slatted benches, *babushki* gossip. Old *stariki* play chess. They look like home. But I am utterly lost. In Brooklyn.

"Why here?" I ask. "Where are we?"

Roma takes his time. He parks the bike and helps me to the sidewalk. He brushes tears from my cheeks. The wind, you know. The speed.

"This is Brooklyn. Brighton Beach. Three more blocks and we're at the ocean. I need to look up Benjamin Frame's number. We'll call him, make sure he's home."

The old men on the benches look up, mildly curious. Then someone mutters, "Checkmate," and Roma and I are forgotten.

"You've never been to Brighton Beach?" he asks, not quite a question. There's a slow chill in my brain when he says it. My mother's less-than-clear directions to dance *even on the boardwalk of Brighton Beach*.

"Your mother lived here." He jerks his head. "Down that way. On Brighton Beach Avenue. She lived there for many years. With Georgi."

"After her father died," I supply. Then I correct myself. "*Ubili*. After her father was killed."

There is a pause. A little boy appears from nowhere, chasing pigeons.

"I need to speak to her," I say.

"Georgi will call as soon as she is released. There are formalities—documents, payments. Plus, it's after midnight there. I think we will hear from them by morning," he answers.

"I want to know now," I say.

He's frozen. Reluctant.

"Spit on midnight, Roma. Call him!"

He shakes his head.

"Lana. Think. We need to know. We need to know for sure."

That shuts me up. Now it's Roma who has doubts. I didn't expect that.

"When I said that Georgi is competent, that he's a powerful man capable of anything. I never meant, you know, capable of . . ." He searches for a word. "But if there is any truth to what you are thinking—that he has been . . . that he has overstepped in his interest. We need to know that first."

"How do we do that?"

"Gosha's house is five minutes from here."

"Well, that's convenient," I say, wary.

"He has four apartments and six buildings in Manhattan," explains Roma. "But his home is still Brighton Beach. If I go there I can find out for sure."

His home is still Brighton Beach. How strange. Georgi and Benjamin, both still here in Marina's once-home. I have the spooky feeling that she still lingers as well.

"So just let me get you to your father, where you will be safe. And then . . ."

"No."

"No what?"

"No. Yes. You're right. First we find out. Benjamin Frame can wait. He's waited this long."

"So . . ."

"So, let's go to Gosha's." I shiver as I say it. It's cooler down here by the ocean. Brooklyn still chafes at spring, forcing its clouds lower. Roma is parking the bike.

"I need to get the key to Georgi's place," he says, "and you need to sit down a minute. Have you even eaten today?"

I'm too tired to argue. I follow him across the street and up a tiny pathway to a crumbling set of stairs leading to a screen door. Cold now. I'm cold. When Roma ushers me into the mist of a soup-infused kitchen and shouts, "Mama, I've brought a guest," his voice is ten years younger.

Brighton Beach, I understand, is everyone's home.

IT TAKES JUST ONE bowl of borscht. Just one plate of stuffed peppers. Just his mother's gentle hand—first on his head, then on the tea cozy, then on a thin plastic plate of gingerbread cookies and then on his head again. It takes just one burst of his father's laughter, which turns to a rattling cough. It takes a single glance between the wife and son, shared in response.

It doesn't take much to warm my chill. Just something deeper than my own drama. In this kitchen occupied by one mother, one father, one son, I feel the plain truth. This is a family as right as its simple math.

Roma's father gets up from the table and opens the door to let in a tiger-striped cat. They engage in a conversation that began long before I arrived in Brooklyn.

—*And you think you deserve to be fed, I suppose, coming home late to dinner.*

—*Mwal*

—*That's no excuse, you mincing devil.*

—*Mwal*

—You might have at least cleaned the street off your feet before waltzing into mother's kitchen, you insolent beastie. Oh, please—my lady, my baryshnya—*allow me to offer you a hankie for your paws.*

—Mwal

—And will it be herring for you tonight, my lady? Or perhaps you'd prefer some of the calf liver I spent half my wages on? And I suppose you'd like caviar to start, you insufferable striped monster.

—Mwal

Now the cat is eating, her servant retired to the other room. Roma's mother is hovering, wanting me to eat more. She's a head shorter than Roma and dressed in a housecoat covered in peacocks. Her name, Zinaida, doesn't fit. She is smaller than her name, softer than the letters involved.

"Mama, we need to go," he says gently. "I'll bring her back later, you can feed her all you want."

He gives her a peck on the cheek and puts his bowl in the sink.

"I'll just be a minute," he says to me.

"Roma is a good boy," Zinaida begins, not three seconds after he's out the door. "It's nice to have him home for dinner. He's always so busy. Comes and goes like . . ." She reaches for another dish and the right analogy.

"The wind," she finishes at the same time as I say, "the cat."

Zinaida laughs. "The cat! Yes, that's right. So many nights I've left his dinner on that shelf." She nods her

head at the high cabinet. "Where the cat can't get at it."
She laughs again, her smile lingering.

"It's his job?" I ask. "That keeps him so busy?"

"Who's to say? He has many things. Jobs. Studies.
Concerts."

She's silent. It occurs to me that Roma's mother hasn't
asked anything about me. He had introduced me as:
"Lana. She's new to Brooklyn."

His parents didn't ask for more information. If his
mother is curious, she doesn't show it.

"He takes us, from time to time," she says. "You
know, to the theater. He'll come home with a new dress,
a new coat. 'Hurry, Mama,' he'll say 'there's a car out
front.' And off we go."

She stacks bowls on the counter. I find a towel and
dry them.

"You've been to Lincoln Center?" she asks.

I nod. "Once or twice."

"I do love the one with the atrium full of balustrades,
you know? The one where you look up and up and
expect Italian maidens and princes and courtiers with
their lutes. What do you call them . . . minstrels."

I smile. Aladdin's cave. I have an unbidden image of
Roma in open sleeves and a turban.

"But that's Roma's world."

"The ballet, you mean."

She nods, wipes her hands on her apron. "Well, the
ballet, I suppose, is a perk. Or maybe just homework.
Georgi Levshik has tried hard to make it Roma's passion, I think. But . . ."

I wait. To hear what Roma's real passion might be.

"Oh—and he's an expert. A real expert, that Georgi. Or at least he carries himself that way. Roma sometimes teases. Says it doesn't take much to remember a bunch of ballets. He says, 'Mama, they're all fairy tales. I learned them from you in the cradle.'"

"I guess he's right about that," I say.

"Oh, sure. *Sleeping Beauty. Rusalka. Swan Lake. Cinderella*—fairy tales, of course. The princess and the shepherd. The magic curse. The happy ending."

The maiden sacrificed in an ancient pagan ritual. Betrayed by her friends. Guilty of near-deaths and other debacles.

"No. The ballet, that's Georgi Levshik's doing," says Zinaida. "Mr. Levshik is a special friend. He recognized Roma himself. Understood that Roma's is a different talent."

Kidnapping maidens? Sabotaging sacrifices? Motorcycle repair?

"You mean as an escort?" I ask. I've used the Russian word that is less loaded, more innocent. The word that means that Roma's value comes from his loyalty, his commitment, his camaraderie. These are Soviet terms that I expect Zinaida to understand.

"Oh no," she answers. She turns and looks at me. "Hasn't he played for you?"

"Play what?" I ask.

"Well, his horn, of course."

"No," I laugh. The thought is absurd. "Which horn is that?"

She blinks.

"I thought you must be here to hear him play. His trumpet."

I look at her blankly.

Just then Roma's father stumbles into the room, a puzzled look on his face.

"Lana Dukovskaya?" he asks. "Is that your name?"

I nod.

"You're on the news."

The television camera sweeps across Lincoln Center at night, sparkling with golden light, shimmering with silhouettes. An announcer is speaking in rapid Russian:

> . . . *remains in critical condition at nearby Roosevelt Hospital. Meanwhile, the Bolshoi troupe is scheduled for another three performances in New York. Including an encore presentation tomorrow night of The Rite of Spring, a solo debuted today to a standing ovation by Lana Dukovskaya, the rising star whose celebrated ascent may well come to a crashing finale if these allegations . . .*

For a minute, I'm tempted to laugh at the tabloid treatment: me—a celebrated rising star, and at the media's ignorance: it's not *The Rite of Spring* that's a solo, it's the Danse Sacrale. But then I'm gripped by the realization of what else has been said: *these allegations.*

"It was first on RNR—Russian news," says Roma's father, waving the remote. "That's where I heard it first, before I came to tell you," he explains. "They said that your mother is under arrest in Moscow and she denies the charges that she attacked the director and this poor girl in New York . . . what was her name?"

He's rewinding the news to five minutes ago. I watch my mother file out of Butyrskaya prison backward into an overexposed city.

"Nina," I answer him softly.

"*Da*, Nina." He stops the remote and presses PLAY. "They're calling it a 'vendetta on pointe' and a 'soloist squabble.'"

We watch my mother led out of a police van and into the prison. She looks vacant, oblivious to the two German shepherds straining on a short leash next to her. Then it is the exterior of the Bolshoi, footage from last year's gala with Pavel holding court among trustees, and all the while, poison from the announcer:

Forty-six-year-old Marina Dukovskaya, a former Bolshoi ballerina who danced in the corps de ballet in the 1990s has been charged with orchestrating last week's attack on the artistic director of the Bolshoi, Pavel Vartukh and another dancer, Daniela Mitrokhin. Dukovskaya has denied any wrongdoing, saying that her only crime was to allow her daughter to join the esteemed dance company one year ago.

The reporter cuts quickly to my mother, wan in the prison lighting: *"I fear for my daughter's safety,"* she says, a catch in her voice.

But RNR has learned from a source within the Bolshoi, that Dukovskaya's daughter, Lana Dukovskaya, is in fact alive and well and enjoying great success in New York City, where today she performed the solo meant to be danced by Nina Oleynikova, who has been hospitalized after a suspected poisoning.

That source confirms that Dukovskaya had been secretly rehearsing the solo in advance of the New York tour, as can be seen in this exclusive footage . . .

I hold my breath. It can, indeed, be seen. By me, by Roma's parents and by everyone watching RNR— whether in Moscow or in Brighton Beach. They are seeing me on the stage, lit by a single spotlight, dancing to a darkened Bolshoi Theatre. They are seeing me just one week ago, heedless of all but my Danse Sacrale, compliments of "a source within the Bolshoi." The audio is poor, the lighting poorer. As the video zooms in to nail me, the resolution slips and shudders. When it comes back into focus, it shows not just me. It shows me and Marina. The reporter pounces:

And not alone. It would appear that Marina Dukovskaya, though she may tonight be worried about her daughter's safety . . . was, as of a week ago, more worried about her daughter's solo in The Rite of Spring . . .

"My God," I whisper. Spring just got crueler.

Roma is behind me, holding my jacket. "Time to go, Lana."

ROMA PARKS THE MOTORCYCLE a block from Georgi's house, a whitewashed brick bungalow hiding on a quiet corner behind an overgrown hedge. He had said it was modest, and it is. It is also ringed with surveillance cameras and under a double armor of security codes. Roma knows them all.

I watch him gain entrance, a professional.

Inside, I glance around, expecting the same glitz and ornate uselessness that typifies the homes of our Moscow millionaires. But there is none of it. There's clutter and dust and drawn blinds. In a small room on the left, there are bookshelves that are clearly used—their contents stacked haphazardly in mid-use: these are necessary books, not a show of brainpower. In a smaller room to the right, there is a table laden with candlesticks, a chessboard and newspapers. I spy several empty wine bottles beneath the table. It looks more like the den of a scholar than of some ruthless oligarch.

"Upstairs," says Roma. "His office is upstairs."

Between the two rooms is a staircase, at the top of which hangs a large framed portrait: A soft-focus beauty radiating the confidence of a woman for whom a camera is never candid. A star who is always in the spotlight. Svetlana Dukovskaya, my grandmother. Roma is halfway up the stairs, but I stumble. I'm Aladdin, afraid of his treasure.

"Do you want to wait for me down there?" he asks.

I shake my head and follow him up the stairs and into a small room at the back of the house. He closes the door behind us. There is a large desk bearing a small laptop. There are filing cabinets and the sort of glass-fronted bookcase that graces every Russian home that has never been renovated. I step forward and scan the spines of the dozen binders stacked upright on the shelves: R-MEX LTD., ALLIED HOLDINGS, RUS-MORTGAGE INC., TRAN-SEURO ESTATES. I run my fingers against the embossed letters, the source of Georgi's power and money. It feels inconsequential. English phrases run through my head: *loaded gun, empty threat, shell game, shell company*.

Roma sits at the desk and turns on the computer. It's a complicated process. Georgi's laptop is as guarded as his Brighton Beach home.

He pulls headphones from a drawer and spends several minutes lost in the computer. I turn my attention back to the shelves. There, above the binders in a row of picture frames, are all the Dukovskys: Georgi and Svetlana manning a paddleboat in Gorky Park; Georgi and Viktor brandishing bottles and skewers of shish kebab; Marina sitting on the hood of a beat-up family car parked outside the *dacha* of my dreams. And there I am, too—my headshot, carefully cut from the Bolshoi Academy graduation announcement. A phalanx of photographs, almost all of them faded.

My vanguard, I think. *My family*.

I turn back to the desk and find Roma's eyes locked on me. He nods once. It seems to hurt him to do so.

"Tell me," I say.

"You were right."

"What did you find?"

"Let me explain."

"Please do."

"The accident. The one in Moscow . . ."

"On Rublevskoye," I clarify. "The attack on Daniela."

"It wasn't supposed to be Daniela. It was supposed to be Vartukh." Roma hesitates. "The hit man. He's Gosha's man."

The confirmation leaves me momentarily deaf. I put my hands on the desk and bow my head to the mute roar in my ears. Roma's doubt is not doubt. He's telling me this. He knows.

I don't lift my head. I don't raise my eyes. I just listen as Roma explains to me that Georgi Levshik had a long-standing arrangement with Pavel Vartukh. One that was good, "mutually beneficial," even "mostly legal" . . . until recently. Something had happened over the past year, he said, that spoiled their relationship. And when it went bad, he said, it went worse; and when it went worse, Georgi lost his head.

I get it. Vartukh had played chicken with Gosha. That's why he passed me over for the tour. Gosha retaliated.

"Understand, Lana, Gosha is without a doubt one of the top five benefactors of the Bolshoi, and he has been for twenty years or more. He's earned a certain authority. He's owed some deference."

I shake my head, sick to my stomach. "No. No, don't

even start with the crap about what Gosha is *owed*. And
don't tell me about the alpha dogs in the Bolshoi. You
think I've never seen one piss on the stage? But to do
what he did? To maim?"

Roma, too, looks unwell. There are dark circles under
his eyes. "It was a botched job. Vartukh was the target,
and he was just supposed to, you know, shake him up.
Threaten him. Gosha was sending him a message. That's
how they send messages in Moscow—you know that.
When Gosha learned she had been hurt . . ." Roma waves
at the computer. "It's right here. He installed this crazy
voice recognition program and the call is all here."

"Show me."

Roma pulls the headphones from the jack and turns
the volume up.

"This is the next morning," he explains. "The morn-
ing he learned that the girl was badly hurt and that
Vartukh was not. This is Georgi when he is at his worst.
When he has made a mistake and can't admit it."

"The girl has a name," I say. "Her name is Daniela."

I lean across Roma and hit PLAY. Poor software, auto-
correcting and a disconnected robotic voice render the
message almost comical, wide of the fury I know was
in Georgi's voice when he realized the damage he had
done:

—*Do you not understand difference beeteen mayhem
and message?*

—*Georgi Ivan-oh-bitch . . . it was dark.*

—*Dark? Dark. You thick-head sunflower? Darker
than inside of uris ascann when uris head is shoved upon*

it? So dark that you drive blind into a weeping world of shit? Did I not say this is a message? A message—not a man's laughter?

—*Da, Georg. You said just that, but* . . .

—*But nut, you sad sack. So here are my last words: you get money to that girl's family or you can expectorate some new friends in prison who will tissue a thing or two about making mistakes in the dark. Do you understand me?*

—*Da, Georgi Ivan-oh-bitch.*

That's the end.

"This is how you got to New York," Roma says quietly, tapping the screen. "And this is how we will clear your name. I'll take it to the police myself."

I'm numb.

Roma pulls a thumb drive from his coat pocket. He stutters something. I look at him stupidly. What is he asking? "Nina. Nina . . . she's the strawberry blonde? Wide face, full lips?"

I nod. Nina. Nina, too. Another of Gosha's botched jobs. *Man's laughter*—that was how the cyborg voice had said it—manslaughter. Stupid, bullying big shots. Laughter. Tears. All the same to the men who peg their happiness on someone else's hard luck.

"I'm so sorry, Lana. I'm sure it's very painful."

It's not painful. It's pathetic. I thought I was the whistle-blower. I thought I was the righteous. I thought I was the better dancer and that my stage was the high ground. But I was wrong. I'm just another bought ballerina. And Daniela and Nina are the roadkill on my high ground.

This is what I'm about to say to Roma and his sympathy. But then I look at him. His face is stricken. I'm bitter, yes. But Roma is devastated.

He picks up the phone. "I'm calling the police. I'm turning him in."

"Wait," I say.

My mind is clear again, but it is in two places. They are both places Vartukh has been. Outside a sushi restaurant on Rublevskoye highway and inside a bar on upper Broadway.

"Vartukh must have known what that motorcycle meant. He knew it wasn't some racist fan of the Bolshoi. He knew it was Georgi Levshik, with an ax to grind. He told me so himself. He said Georgi is a *man with bad fucking aim*. The story about the Russian nationalist? That *Bolshoi for the Russians* business? That was Anna's spin. She's the spin master. Vartukh told me that, too. I didn't listen, but he told me that Anna had taken control. It was her choice to pass me over for the tour, not Vartukh's. Just like, after the accident, it was her choice to bring me."

I cover my eyes with one hand, trying to understand what it was he was telling me yesterday: *The Dukovskaya show.*

"Vartukh is crooked and a little depraved, yes. But Anna Arkhipova . . ."

I open my eyes and they land on the shelf of photographs. There is another frame hiding behind Marina on the hood of the car. I reach for it. Two young women, smiling, arms linked, posing in front of the Bolshoi

Theatre, squinting in winter sunshine. One has long dark hair and a purple suede coat—Marina. The other, blonde, tucked into a knit cap. I look closer. Anna Arkhipova.

"Anna Dmitrievna has her own agenda," I conclude.

"And her own ax to grind," a voice adds from the door, which is now open. Who would have thought that he could be so quiet coming up the stairs? My wheezing, scheming Dyadya Gosha, who should have landed in Moscow only hours ago . . .

Roma is on his feet. But I'm quicker. I'm in his face, brandishing the photo of teenage Marina Dukovskaya and Anna Arkhipova.

"Did you negotiate with her, too, Gosha?" I shout, grabbing his silk shirt, damp with sweat. "Did you reroute your 'Svetlana Fund' payments to land in her account? To land Nina in the hospital?"

Then a whole slew of accusations: "*monster, liar, kidnapper, psychopath*"—delivered with the emphasis of the framed photograph. The glass breaks, his forehead bleeds. And still I beat him with the shattered frame.

"*Spokoyno*, Lana," he growls. "Stay calm."

Roma, in English, warns him that it's too late for that. We are all shouts and deafness.

"Listen to me," Georgi is saying, "Listen to me . . ."

But I'm still shrieking. "You sick, sad man. You said you would fix this but you broke it! You've ruined everything! You've ruined me, just like you ruined my mother!"

Marina. Guard dogs. Butyrskaya.

"And why are you here? You said you would . . . Dear God. You lied about that, too! Where's Marina? Who's . . . ?"

Still I am pummeling him. Georgi twists my arm behind my back, turning outrage to pain.

"Don't touch her, Gosha!" Now Roma. "Enough!"

I'm thrown back and slam my hip on the desk. Roma, too, steps back, blocking me. But Georgi is on the floor. I can see the black trace of Roma's fist below Georgi's eye. And my work, too—the gash above it.

Georgi sits slowly. He raises his hand and wipes away blood.

"I am here," he says calmly, "because I need to make a call. An on-the-record call. I need, yes, to call Anna Arkhipova and let her know that she botched the job."

"LET'S BACK UP. START at the beginning. When you bought a ticket to Moscow, but didn't use it."

Roma is standing, his fists clenched. Gosha is lying on the small couch by the wall. I'm bandaging his head. The wound is deep. And behind his ear, two contusions where he hit the door jamb and then the floor.

Gosha's speech is slow and his story confused. He had begun to unpack an explanation. He hadn't poisoned Nina, he said. He had gotten there on time. Well, not quite on time. But better late than never, he had said.

Then he had risen from the floor and started patting the pockets of his suit coat. "Fingerprints," he was muttering, "toxicity." But I saw him swaying, ready to fall. I told him to lie down.

Now I'm waiting for sense.

I bite my tongue. I know that time is against us, but if we fight it, we lose. Then again, I don't know who "we" are.

"Why did you buy a ticket, Gosha?" Roma's voice is hard.

"Because I fully intended to fly to Moscow," he answers. "As soon as I learned that Marina had been arrested, I booked a flight. I didn't need to, of course. I know that."

He shifts his gaze from Roma to me. I'm too close; his eyes cross and then close. "I could have fixed it with one call." He grunts. "Two maybe. It's six A.M. in Moscow. She won't spend another night in custody, I promise."

I glance at Roma. He's staring at Georgi, willing him to explain.

"You've heard of a pretext?" mumbles Gosha. "I've waited fifteen years for a pretext. I wanted to see her— Marina. I wanted her to see me when she walked out. I wanted to hear her say thank you."

"For what?" I ask. I mean it honestly, not cruelly.

"Well." He has no pat answer. "You have a point."

"So why didn't you go?" Roma asks again.

"That's the funny part. You see, I was at the airport. And who do I see being escorted through security and to the same gate?"

He waits. As though we will answer.

"Pavel Vartukh. That's who." Gosha chuckles, coughs, winces. "He was in worse shape than me right now, I'll tell you. But he recognized me. And he slipped his minder, a big guy busy playing video games on his phone. Says he's going to the can. I follow him in. He was half in his cups. Blotto on something. Something not just, you know . . ." Gosha flicks his chin with a finger, the Russian shorthand for drinking. He's silent for too long.

"Gosha?" I prod.

Georgi's eyes flick open. "He tells me that Arkhipova's the one who ratted Marina. I was impressed, if you wanna know. I underestimated that snake with tits. I shouldn't have. Because she had a whole mess of rats to let loose."

I tuck the bandage into its wrap. He snatches my hand and kisses it. "*Spasibo, dochka.*" I bite my tongue again. *I'm not your dochka.* I leave his side and begin picking up the glass on the floor. The glass that had frozen my mother and Anna in a moment in time.

"She used to be your mother's friend," says Gosha, watching me. "Anya, she was, then, little Anya, Anyushka. Marya would mention her in her letters. How much she had changed when she returned to Moscow. How much everything had changed. How brutal ballerinas could be, when they see their fragile future. 'Anya' had become Anna. She had become cold and she had become fierce. She saw Marya as a threat. A rival."

Ah, yes. Friends who are rivals. I'm familiar with this.

"Anna went after Marina with everything she had. First just *slova, vzglyadi.* That awful thing that women can do with one word, one look. But then smears and then lies. She was vicious. She was cruel. It was a hard time for Russia and for the ballet—everyone broke. Nothing certain. But Anna did not handle it with grace. She resented everything about Marina and her return."

He pauses. Roma is impatient, but I signal him to wait. I want to hear this.

"Your mother didn't have the strength for new enemies. She wasn't the fighter you are, Lana. She retreated. Surrendered. Covered her head with her hands. And I couldn't bear it. So I fought for her."

"What did you do?"

"I used what I had to get Danilov, the director at the time, to put her in her place."

"Money."

"Nope. Didn't have that then."

"So . . ."

"Svetlana. I used Svetlana."

Now I wince. There's a shard of glass in my hand.

"I had always suspected that he was the one who turned Sveta in, you see. Danilov was as in love with her as any of us. I suspected that Sveta confided in him and told him she planned to defect with her family. I imagine he just couldn't let her go."

I glance at Roma, who is eyeing his bleeding boss with something between anger, confusion, and concern. I process the words.

"You're saying that Arkady Danilov, Vartukh's predecessor, gave my grandmother to the KGB?" I ask after a moment.

"That is what I suggested to him," Gosha answers. His voice is clearer now, more lucid. "I told him I could take him down with the files I had found. And he begged. Begged like a sinner before the saints. So I guess I was right."

I sit on the floor, my legs weak. "Were there really files?" I ask.

"None. We . . . we pretty much confirmed it." Gosha hesitates slightly. He doesn't know that I know about "we." That I know about Benjamin Frame. "But I told Danilov there were. I said I had them and that they named him as the informant. I told him that I could close the case, declare her dead, stop all the investigations. If he would just put that damn Anna in her place."

Bozhe, I breathe. *My God*. The legendary Danilov, the darling, the symbol of a golden era. The antithesis of Vartukh. But no—he was a crooked one, too. *They sold all the gold*, that's what my mother had said.

"And Marina found out," I say.

"And Marina found out," Gosha agrees.

His eyes are moist. He dabs at them with his tie. "Marina found out. Marina quit. She quit the ballet and she quit me. Danilov retired. Anya arrived and clawed her way to the top. Dyadya Gosha lost."

The room is thick with knowledge that helps nothing.

I rise and open a window.

I'm standing with my back to him, thinking of my mother, who won't fight anything but the truth. And then I think of Nina, downed but not dead—Anna Arkhipova's "botched job."

I say, "I don't care who started this fight. You have to win it, Dyadya Gosha."

. . .

IN THEORY, WE HAVE already won. That's what
Gosha says. He says we can prove it: Anna Arkhipova
took advantage of the Rublevskoye attack to pay back
an old grievance. It was a long time coming. It had been
twenty-five years since she helped take down Danilov
and promote Vartukh, and the moment Pavel faced
his own fragile future in the guise of a reckless BMW
motorcycle, she cashed in those debts.

"She was setting you up every step of the way,"
Gosha explains. "Vartukh played along until he didn't,
and that's when she sent him home."

"Setting me up," I repeat. "Nina . . ."

"That's right," says Gosha in the voice you use to
encourage a toddler trying out first steps. "Nina. Anna
figured a dead girl in New York would be more convincing than a roughed-up one in Moscow. She could pin
one on you and one on your mother. And I can tell you
right now, that's what she would have gotten if I hadn't
hauled ass back from the airport to save that poor girl."

Gosha struggles to sit. He does not look like much of
a savior.

"You saved her?" I repeat, trying to understand. He
doesn't answer immediately. He pats his suit coat and
pulls out a piece of paper.

"I've got the toxicity report from the hospital. Dinitrophenol, for God's sake. It's a supplement, you can
only buy it online. It burns fat by turning your body
into a furnace. Nobody has it except aging Russian

ballerinas who somehow managed to survive the stuff while it was still unregulated. Them and bodybuilders. My guy's already got it. Snatched it from her bag."

"What guy?" asks Roma quietly.

"Whatshisname. Angry Birds guy."

"Ivan!" I exclaimed. "That's not your guy, Gosha. That's Anna's guy. He was my damn watchdog all morning."

"And did a good job of it, no?"

"A good job of keeping me locked in my room!"

"A good job of keeping you alive," Gosha spits back. "I wasn't taking any chances. How the hell did I know how many ballerinas that witch was going to poison? I hadn't put it all together yet."

His hands shake and the report drops to the floor. I get the feeling he still hasn't put it all together. I get the feeling that no one is saved. I think of the pills I kicked from her suitcase. My fingerprints all over them. I think of Ivan, delivering me to the lobby. Into the clutches of a poisoner. I tell Georgi what I'm thinking.

"Well, of course I let you go. I knew her game then." Gosha shoots a fiery eye at Roma. "She wanted you to appear in Nina's place. That was the optics piece. The one for public consumption. C'mon. You saw the news."

Roma and I are still processing.

"You did see the news, didn't you?" says Gosha. His voice is weak again, heading into a slalom of slurs. "So I let her play it out and now . . . now all we gotta do is . . . I gotta call up Anna and tell her. I tell her— you, *Anya dorogaya*, botched that job. Nina will live and will hang you, Anya, my dear. I got the diniph-whatsitcalled,

and I'll hang you, too. Hang you by the hangidy ass
zhopa. Anya, *moya zhopa.* My poisonous . . . Unless,
how about we make a deal?" He waggles his head and
waves to the computer on the desk. "We get her on the
tape thingy there and then she's hung for certain."

"You hurt your head," I say. "You're not making
sense." I turn to Roma. "We should take him to the hospital."

"No hospital," says Gosha, momentarily lucid. "I
can't work in the hospital. I can't trap this snake from
the hospital."

And then he lies back down and is quiet.

"Gosha," I say. "Gosha!"

He's out cold.

ROMA CALLS THE HOSPITAL. Not the one nearby
where, by rights, we should be taking Georgi. He calls
Roosevelt Hospital on Tenth Avenue in Manhattan,
down the street from Lincoln Center. Nina, he's told, is
still in intensive care and that's all the information available. I lean into Roma's shoulder and listen.

"The patient is a visiting artist. A foreigner. Unless
you are an immediate relation or . . ." Her voice is gentle, encouraging.

"Can you please just tell me what time she was admit-
ted and by whom?"

"Sir . . ."

"Please. Please. She's a friend. I just need to know
how she got to the hospital. Did she come on her own?
Just tell me that. I won't ask any more. She's a friend."

"Are you a member of the press?"

"No. A friend."

I listen to this convincing concern and wonder if this is Roma's talent. The one that Georgi Levshik discovered and cultivated: knowing how to appeal to women. How to get them to divulge information. How to get them on the back of his bike. I'd believe him. That he was her friend.

There's a pause on the other end of the phone. Even I can hear the nurse debate her instincts.

"She was brought in a police car. She was found outside her hotel. In an alley. She had jumped from a fire escape. She had a broken leg and a temperature of one-oh-four and her kidneys were failing when she arrived. She's a hell of a trouper. She has a police sergeant at her door and she's under careful monitoring."

I've underestimated Nina. Who manages to escape a locked hotel room and climb down a fire escape while in a metabolic fever? Nina Oleynikova, it turns out. Not a craven stooge. A trouper.

Roma thanks the woman and hangs up.

"Police guard," I say, to hide my shame. "Way to go, New York's finest. I'm impressed."

"Gosha's," he says.

"No."

"*Sporim*. I'll bet you. I'll call back and ask her to put Sergeant Boris Makarov on the phone. He's the most upright cop on the West Side. And now he's sitting outside Nina's hospital room."

I think about this. Gosha and all his guys. His

toxicologist in the hospital, his police cruising the premises of the hotel for a half-dead girl, his cop at Nina's door and his Ivan, newly conscripted and on the fly. Yet it's Roma here who knows the combination to his house, the code to his computer, and, if I still believe him, the mysteries of my family.

Which raises an obvious question.

"Why didn't he call you, Roma?" I ask. "Why didn't Gosha send you to break down the door and rescue Nina and rifle Anna's suitcase? Why didn't he tell you to watch out for me, make sure I didn't get a dose of fever, too?"

The blood drains from his face. "Because we've all had our moments of doubt," he says. "And he had his this morning."

I watch him closely. I see a man who I want to believe has never, would never . . . but who, I know, probably has . . . and would. Especially for me.

"Where were you this morning, Roma?" I ask. "At sunrise, like you promised."

He sighs. "I was across the street from you. With Nina Oleynikova."

FOURTEEN
SHEEPSHEAD BAY

This time I travel by taxi.

It is closing in on eleven o'clock and I am headed east to Sheepshead Bay. It's just a few minutes away, Roma has assured me.

"Five twenty-two Coleridge Street in Sheepshead Bay," he told the driver. "Just off the marina." Then he gave me Gosha's cell phone. "Call me as soon as you arrive."

I'm not sure what I will say. I mean, I know, more or less, what I will say to Benjamin Frame. I'll say I've brought Bolshoi baggage to his door. But I'm not sure what I will say to Roma. He's got his own baggage.

Roma, it turns out, did wait for me all night. Or, at least, was the first customer at the diner across the street when it opened at sunrise. He waited, he said, until seven and then sent me a text.

Nice day for a ride.

The response, he said, was slow to come: Where are you? But shortly after that, he said, Nina emerged from the hotel. "She came right across the street. Straight into the diner. She sat down next to me at the counter."

She came with a message: "Lana's going to perform today. She's going to dance the solo. Anna Dmitrievna said you should let Georgi Ivanovich know, so he can be there."

I asked Roma how she seemed. How did Nina, who knew I had been dragged kicking and screaming from the lobby the night before, seem when she delivered this news?

"Fine. Happy. A little giddy even. Until . . ."

"Until?"

"Until I said that I was glad it had all worked out. That you had been concerned for her. That's when she changed."

"Suspicion?" I asked.

"Guilt," he said.

I thought of the scene in the lobby. Nina's distress. Anna's dismissal: *It will be better in the morning.*

Hell. I believed her, didn't I? Maybe not in the morning but by the time the curtain rose I did. Why shouldn't Nina have thought the same thing? Why shouldn't she have woken up thinking that everything was better? That I was going to perform the Danse Sacrale and forgive her moment of weakness? Why shouldn't Nina have been convinced that I had momentarily, indeed, gone rogue, lost my head . . . and needed the strong hand of leadership? She's Russian, after all. We believe in leadership. We trust in iron fists. It's our weakness.

"She ordered a large orange juice," continued Roma. "To go. Said it was for you. I offered to pay. I insisted, in fact. I told her to tell you it was from me and that . . ."

He stopped talking then. We put it together. Anna had squared Roma in her trap for good measure. Along with the DNPx in Nina's system, there would be orange juice. Among the text messages on my phone, there would be these:

—Nice day for a ride.

—Where are you?

—Across the street.

—Enjoy the orange juice. I hope it hits the spot.

—Yes. Nina will enjoy it.

"I just let it go. I mean, I wasn't going to make a big deal about orange juice, you know," Roma had said. "But now, even if Nina survives, Anna has a lot of circumstantial evidence."

"Including a whole bottle of dinitrophenol with my fingerprints all over it."

That's when he insisted I leave. "She's going to want you in custody before this thing unravels. The news will have pictures of us both running from the press, and she will use it. She let you go because she knows how to find you. She knows you're with me and she knows who I am. That was Nina's message: *tell Georgi Ivanovich.* Lana, you can't be here."

"So come with me."

But Roma wouldn't leave Gosha.

He pulled out his phone and scrolled. "When I left the diner I sent him a text." He showed me: Nina confirmed. Lana dances tonight. "My guess is he misinterpreted it. He knew Arkhipova's plan by then and he thought I had somehow been used by her. That's why he didn't call me with directions. He doubted me, just as I doubted him."

"But you had reason to," I had insisted. "Gosha was responsible for what happened to Daniela. You had nothing to do with Nina." *Except you bought her the orange juice that would be her undoing.*

"Trust, I think you will agree, slips easily," he'd said.

He's right of course. I've spent the last 24 hours in a world of razor-edged loyalties. They are thin and very sharp. They let you trust just until they slip and you are cut.

Roma insisted on staying with Gosha, getting him to the hospital if necessary.

I wonder if we've killed the old man.

I glance out the window. We are driving under elevated train tracks that put a roof over the darkness. Everywhere are the signs that Russia lives here: *apteka, gastronom, knizhniy, nochnoy klub.* Night shoppers crowd in bunches in brightly lit storefronts and I can read them, too. What a strange place, this Brighton Beach. A mini-Russia on an urban beach, stuck in an era I recognize, but don't remember. Marina's era. Little Marina, that is. Marya's world. Alongside with Starbucks, CVS and yes, Bank of America.

Above the stores and restaurants on Brighton Beach Avenue rise five floors of another night life: Families around the table, children in front of the TV, cats cleaning their paws in view of the elevated subway trains.

My mother lived in one of these apartments, I think. My grandfather was killed in one of these nightclubs. The thoughts flit past as quickly as the stripes of open sky between dense blocks of apartment buildings. I roll down the window. It smells of the ocean and weather that's heavier than spring. In Brighton Beach it could be any season.

When the taxi emerges from under the elevated tracks, I am looking at the marina that splits the bottom of Brooklyn in two. Some of the boats in the harbor have festive lights winding up their masts. Others are circled in seagulls, bright white in the dark. We turn right and slow down until we aren't moving at all. The driver turns to look at me.

"Five twenty-two Coleridge Street."

My father lives here. In Sheepshead Bay. Benjamin Frame lives in a house with a front porch pushed back from the street and a back porch looking out onto the marina.

Marina, I think. *Marina.*

The air is thick and moist; a storm is on its way. I feel a few drops of the rain's advance army.

I haven't even closed the door of the car when he comes catapulting out of the house like a cartoon. He is all forward motion and velocity; his legs centripetal and his hair alight. Now he has me in his arms. For the first time in five days, I don't second-guess what is happening. My father has me in his arms.

He has seen the news. Starring me and Roma speeding away from Lincoln Center. And a new development:
"corroborating evidence" of my involvement. A hand-
written mea culpa: *Especially for You, Lana,* tucked
under the half-drunk cup of orange juice in which traces
of DNPx were found. The authorities, said the news,
intend to bring me in for questioning.

It's so absurd I want to laugh.

"Tell me everything," he says.

"Everything's not important," I say. "What's important
is Marina is in prison, Nina is in the hospital, and Gosha is
probably concussed. I'm kind of in deep shit, too."

Benjamin Frame wraps me again in his arms. He
squeezes me so hard I stop breathing. That, too, feels
fine. He looks up and down the block and says, "Let's
go inside."

WE START WITH THE obvious. Marina's cell phone.
Her home phone. The dance school. Nothing. My father
gets on the Internet and pulls up numbers for the Moscow Municipal Police; the Regional Department of
Safety; the Deputy Head of Public Security; the Ministry
of Internal Affairs; and finally Petrovka, 38.

"No, Benjamin," I say. "It's not the Soviet Union anymore. You have to cut to the chase. Find a number for
Butyrskaya Prison."

This time we get an answer. Just not the kind we
need. Only "Dispatcher 35, Butyrka, what's the purpose
of your call?" and "That information is classified. You
must direct it to the Ministry of Internal Affairs."

My father is an expert in atonal polyphony and modularity in early twentieth-century symphonic composition. We are in his kitchen, the unfussy neatness of which tells me that he lives alone. There's a stack of blue exam books on the table. The top one reads: SCALE AND CHROMATIC EXTRAPOLATION IN SYMPHONIC NOMENCLATURE. EXIT THESIS BY M. VERLANGER. SUBMITTED TO PROFESSOR B. FRAME.

"You teach," I say.

"I do," he concurs.

"Not exactly Music 101," I note.

The point is: my father knows an awful lot about a certain esoteric kind of communication. But it is very different from the kind of communication that gets you answers about an inmate in Detention Center 77/2 Department of the Federal Penitentiary Service of Russia for Moscow, Butyrskaya. Benjamin Frame speaks chromatic scales and augmented flats. He speaks Russian, too, yes. But he doesn't speak their language, the language of bureaucratized indifference to justice. He probably never did.

"I'm afraid we need Georgi," he says, hanging up the phone in defeat. He shakes his head, amused by something I don't see. "I never thought I'd hear myself say that again. But this is out of my league. And it is exactly in his. So . . . what did he say he's doing about this?"

"We didn't get that far," I say. Then I explain the situation.

"You attacked him," he says.

"It was blind rage," I reply. "I mean, he pushed me.

Surely you can see that. He pushed me to it. I thought he had tried to kill my two best friends. Two innocent girls. You have no idea what that can do to you."

"Actually . . ." He is rubbing his scalp. That thing I do. Only a little more manic. "Actually, yes, I do know." Again, a flash of unfunny amusement. He stands abruptly and leaves the kitchen.

I hear him knocking around in the other room. Through the open door I see his silhouette against the sliding-glass door that leads out onto the marina. He opens it wide and I smell the tang of a restless night. A silent splinter of lightning throws the room into visibility and I see him walk back to me, his face solemn.

He sits again. "I need to tell you what I didn't have time to tell you last night. I mean, it's a thing that needs time. And we didn't have it. I don't know if we do now. I don't know that we ever will. But it's about Gosha. And it's about the things we do when we are afraid for a friend."

He's holding a photograph. I take it. Another piece of the mosaic of Marina. This one has her squeezed between a young Benjamin Frame and a girl with an impish grin, black bangs and big gold hoops.

"That's Lindsay," he says simply. "She's the friend."

I study the picture. She and my mother are smiling into the camera. Benjamin is smiling just at Marina.

"Back then, when I first met your mother, we were in this same predicament, believe it or not. Georgi was wounded. He was in the hospital. I can see him now, lying there, arm in a sling, front teeth bashed out, laughing at Marya's outrage and scolding her distrust."

Suddenly Ben leans back, clears his throat, hunches his shoulders and growls, "*I'm no angel, thank God. But haven't I done enough without sending your boyfriend to the slammer, Marya?*"

He's doing his Dyadya Gosha impersonation and it's spot-on.

"You know why we needed him?" he continues.

I shake my head.

"We needed him to clear my name."

He holds his hand out for the photo. "Because, like you, I thought that my friend's life was in danger. Lindsay's."

Another sharp ribbon of lightning dances beyond the boats, too far to be heard as Benjamin corrects himself: "No. No. That's not quite right. I *knew* that her life was in danger. She had a gun to her head."

I feel the chill at the nape of my neck. It climbs to my scalp.

"Georgi was there," he says. "He'd been shot. And we needed him to survive to tell the police just what really happened in that room."

He drums his fingers on the table. A complicated rhythm.

"What really happened in that room?" I ask.

From the open door across the house, the last bit of night comes rushing in ahead of the rain.

"It was self-defense," he answers. "Viktor Feodorovich—your grandfather—When he lost his wife, Svetlana, he lost everything. Within a month of arriving here, he began to lose his way. Lose his mind. This one afternoon, it all came to a head. He had a gun, he shot Gosha, and then he held it to the head of an innocent girl, Lindsay. We had no reason to be there, but we were. I had no choice. I didn't mean to kill him. I meant to save someone's life. But I did both. What happened in that room is—I made your mother an orphan."

I take a deep breath. I smell the coming storm. I smell the last mystery in a string of mysteries that have plagued me all my life. I smell the rain that will wash it away.

"You shot my grandfather in the nightclub," I whisper.

"Yes," he says. "I did. And I went to trial and I was exonerated and I followed your mother to Moscow. I vowed to help her move on, but I failed at that, too. That's what I meant last night when I said that there were other things, more tangible than Sveta. There was this. There was Viktor. I killed Marya's father. The cards were just stacked against us. There was too much guilt. Too much loss."

I don't know how long we sit in silence. Every second could be a year. Decades are passing in Benjamin Frame's kitchen, but the clock says it's just after midnight. He is the first to acknowledge it.

"Let's come back to the present, Lana. You are here and that is like a miracle for me. That means everything."

He stands and crosses to the stove. He picks up the teakettle. "Let's try to avoid more guilt, shall we? Let's try to cut losses."

"Yes," I say, still looking at the clock. My mind is not

here in this kitchen, yet it registers the time and the fact that I've still not called Roma.

My father is filling the kettle at the sink and looking out the window. The sound of running water and pouring rain drown out the sound of what he sees.

"That boy. The trumpet player. The one who brought you to the Vanguard. To me."

"Roma," I say, thinking he's asking for his name. Somewhere in the back of my mind, Roma has a last name too. But I never learned his patronymic, his father's name. I look up at my own father, gazing through rain out onto the street.

"Yes, Roma," he says. "He works for Gosha?"

"He does," I say. "Or did."

"Well, he's here now."

THERE ARE THREE OF us sitting at the table.

"I took him to Coney Island Hospital," says Roma. "It's not far. He's in stable condition. He'll be fine."

"How did you get him there?" I ask, trying to imagine Georgi on the back of Roma's bike.

"Ivan showed up. With the pills, incidentally." Roma pulls a plastic bag from a sodden messenger bag on the floor. I recognize the two bottles. Valium for Vartukh. DNPx for Nina. "I followed them on my bike and came straight here."

Benjamin Frame is pouring tea into three cups.

"You're soaked through," he says. "I'll get you a change of clothes." He throws a glance at me. "And maybe you'd like to get out of your Sacagawea outfit."

I'm still in my costume. I'm still the Chosen One. There are goosebumps all up my arms. They could be from anything. He leaves Roma and me alone in the kitchen.

"How well do you know my father?" I ask.

"I don't. I know his music."

I loop a finger through the handle of the cup in front of me and rotate it slowly.

"What else?"

"I know he plays the Vanguard more than the Blue Note and never does festivals."

"What else?"

"He is a man who lives alone but isn't lonely."

I look up and speak sharply: "What does that mean?"

"That he's a man at peace," says Roma. "I think." Now he is rotating his own cup. "But I could be wrong."

"You know that it was him?" I ask. "He's the one who killed my mother's father."

Roma stretches one hand across the table, palm up.

"Lana, that's not something you could hear from me," is his answer.

"But you knew."

"I did. I do. And now you do, too. If last night, things had gone differently . . ."

"You would have told me?"

"Benjamin Frame would have told you."

I nod. I think, *Yes—it's been eighteen years. What difference does twenty-four hours make?* And I answer my rhetorical question: *everything.*

Because if he had told me last night, I might have

hated him. I might have, like my mother, buried that truth in my palm like a shard of glass and let it fester. But he told me tonight. And tonight, I recognize the burden of bad choices. Of snap judgments that may never be justified.

As if he reads my mind, Roma says, "Gosha will pull through, Lana. And he will do the right thing."

"Says the guy who was ready to turn him in to the police," I say. But his palm is still open and I put mine across it. He wraps his fingers over my knuckles and I answer with a pivot of my wrist. Now our fingers are interlaced. Solid.

Benjamin Frame walks back into the kitchen with flannel shirts and sweatpants. "There's a bathroom in the hall," he says, and then his phone rings. He crosses to the counter, looks at the screen and scowls.

"What is it?" I ask.

"It's you. You are calling me." He holds up the phone. The screen reads Lana.

"Game on," I say. "Anna wants me back."

"Anna?" he asks.

"Anna Dmitrievna Arkhipova. Deputy Director of the Ballet." I say. I can see he hasn't made the connection. Benjamin Frame left the Bolshoi behind twenty years ago. "Anya," I say.

His face clouds. "Ah," he says. "Of course. Of course, Anya."

The phone rings three times. Four times. The silence when it stops is a short sweetness.

My father is still looking at the phone when he says,

"I didn't tell you that I was at the performance today. It was remarkable. Your solo was just remarkable."

I smile. I know.

"I waited for you afterward. But, you know. You didn't emerge."

I did, of course. Like a bat out of hell. Even beat the old folks out of the theater. The ones who already have their coats on when the curtain falls.

"I didn't know, of course, about all this . . ." He waves his hands, indicating all this Bolshoi bullshit.

"And now you are implicated," I say sadly.

"No. No, I don't mean that at all," he says, his voice tight. "I just mean that if I had known . . . I wouldn't have left a message. I wouldn't have left, period."

"But you did," I sigh. "And now Anna knows you're here and she knows I know you're here."

"Anna," mutters Benjamin Frame. "Christ, Anya. When will you stop?"

Roma stands. He pulls at his T-shirt, sticking wet on his chest. "But what's her game?" he says. "If she's calling, then it's the long game. She's not yet told the police how to find us; how to find Lana."

"Because she doesn't have enough," says Benjamin.

I raise my eyebrows. "Enough?"

Benjamin sits down. He pushes away the pile of blue exam books. They cascade to the floor.

"Lana. This is America," he says. "We certainly haven't mastered justice and we have a checkered track record with the whole 'innocent until proven guilty' ideal but we don't arrest young women on the basis of an autographed program and video clips from Moscow, for God's sake."

I look at him. I look at Roma. He's shaking his head. He's less sure. Benjamin's America and Roma's America, I realize, have a two-dimensional intersection. The Village Vanguard is one dimension. Dukovskayas are another. But that third dimension is elusive, and Roma feels it closing in around me.

Now it is his phone that rings. He digs it from his pocket and places it flat on the table. Lana is calling.

I can't stand it. I lunge for it. Both of them stop me. The phone clatters to the floor and I grab my hair in two fists.

"What?" I yell. "Why? We're supposed to let her intimidate us? Make me hide?"

"Don't hide," says my father with certainty. "No hiding, Lana. You are innocent. You are strong. Just like your mother."

It's the only thing I need to hear. The only thing. I am strong. I am innocent. I'm like my mother. That's what my father says.

The clock ticks. It is 12:25 in the morning. When the phone rings again, it's not Benjamin's. It's not Roma's. We all three turn to the sound. My long trench coat, slung over the countertop. It's the phone that Roma gave me to use to tell him I had arrived safely. The one I forgot to use. Gosha's phone.

I jump from the table and pull it from the pocket and, sure enough, it's me. I'm calling every damn person I know in Brooklyn.

Oh, *bozhe*.

Georgi Levshik's plummy voice is talking in my head: *I can't trap this snake from the hospital.*

I'm gripping the phone. Three rings. *I gotta call up Anna and tell her, Anya dorogaya, you botched that job.*

Four rings.

I close my eyes and see red. I am innocent. I am strong. I open them and hit green.

"*Anna Dmitrievna. Dobriy vecher, eto Lana.* I'm glad you called. I'm in Brooklyn. With my uncle. And with my father."

I cast my eyes at Roma and see awe on his face.

"I'm with friends, Anna Dmitrievna, and I won't be coming back to Manhattan until tomorrow. I'll be at the theater by three. And I would be much indebted to you if you could keep the press at bay until then."

FIFTEEN
CONEY ISLAND

Gosha is awake. He is awake, in stable condition and he is laughing.

It's not a loud laugh. In fact, it's hardly audible under the clatter of gurneys and the announcements coming from the speakers in the busy hallways of Coney Island Hospital. But he's laughing. His head bandaged, his arms punched with IVs, and his eyes bloodshot and blackened, Georgi Levshik is laughing at me.

"If you only knew the déjà vu you are giving me right now, *dochka*," he chuckles. "I think it was on this very floor, maybe in this very room, that your mother read me her riot act, thirty years ago. She was an outraged innocent—like you. There I was, still hemorrhaging from the bullet Viktor gave me for my lack of faith, and she put another one in my heart. She blamed me for everything."

"Not everything," I say. "That came later."

His laughter is gone. His smile fades. "Have you heard from her?"

I have. It is what woke me this morning. Before sunrise. And though it woke me from a delicious delirium—sound sleep, Roma's arms, no dreams—I could not have asked for a more welcome sound than Gosha's phone ringing and Marina's worried voice not waiting for a hello.

"*Dyadya Gosha, gde Lana!* Where's my daughter?"

"She phoned this morning," I say. "You were right. She didn't spend another night in jail. They let her go and gave her a ride home and a file that included release papers, an affidavit signed by the Head of Domestic Security, the Chief of Internal Investigations and by the guarantor, Georgi Levshik."

He closes his eyes, his face stronger than proud.

"As well as a ticket to New York, an American visa and a signed declaration of professional misconduct by the department of criminal procedures," I add. "I've never heard of such a thing. That's insane. That doesn't happen."

Gosha smiles again. A kid who's pulled off a magic trick. "You shouldn't doubt me, *dochka*," he says happily.

"She was singing your praises, Marina was. Until I explained it was your own damn fault she was arrested in the first place."

"Now look," he growls, "we've been over this already. Anna Arkhipova—"

"Is a snake with tits," I finish. "Yes. I know. That's

why I'm here. I know how we're going to do this. Trap the snake."

He sits up a bit straighter in the hospital bed, tugs at the tape on his arm. "Okay," he agrees, nodding. "Good. That's good to hear."

I pull up a chair. I'm ready. But he whimpers.

"What is it? Do I need to call the nurse?"

"No," he says, but his voice is weak. "Just tell me— Marina, Marya, does she forgive me?"

I remember her words clearly: *You don't come out of Butyrka a free woman if someone has sent you in to stay. Dyadya Gosha has redeemed himself. That fallen angel.*

But that's not what I tell Georgi.

"She is more forgiving than I am."

He snorts. "It took her long enough."

"And Benjamin Frame, too," I add. "He is, for some reason, willing to defend you."

"Benjamin Frame," he murmurs, his eyes still closed. "Perhaps the only other man as compromised in his love for Marina."

Roma walks in, bearing a tray with breakfast. He puts it down on a cabinet just inside the door. No one suggests that it might be edible.

"So where are we?" he asks.

"We are at the point where we need that recording software," I say. "We are at the point where we lay out a simple chronology. Gosha here calls Anna to spell it all out: Marina is free. Nina's not dead. And Ivan has pocketed proof from her suitcase that she's a poisoner."

Georgi claps his hands. "Perfect. Just as I suggested. Of course it would have been much easier to extract a confession from her if I weren't in a hospital bed."

He rolls his eyes at us, as if we are a couple of naughty puppies that buried his brass knuckles in the backyard. "I'm good, mind you. I can do it. But I am in a goddamn hospital gown."

"Which is why all you do is make this first call," I say. "I take care of the rest."

He scowls. "Lana," he says, "you don't have the experience."

"Spit on experience," I say. "I have a huge stake in this and it's time for you to make room."

He grunts. Roma laughs. I don't have time for any of this.

"You call her now. You tell her I've just left for Lincoln Center. You tell her Marina hopes to make the performance. You tell her you've arranged it, as you have arranged everything. And that nothing will give you greater pleasure than to see Lana perform the Svetlana Variation with Marina in the audience."

The Dukovskaya show, I think. "You tell her, quite simply, that the game is up."

"*Okh, poganka*," breathes Georgi. "You evil child, what are you trying to do? You want her to strangle you bare-handed the minute you arrive at the stage door?"

"More or less," I say, handing him his phone.

He takes it. Georgi Levshik, I discover, has a dimple when he smiles.

• • •

THE CHESS PLAYERS ARE nowhere to be found on the boulevard outside Coney Island Hospital. The sky is clear after last night's rain, brushed as clean as the stage after the final curtain.

Which is to say, not entirely clean.

Arkhipova took the bait. It was startling to have it confirmed, I'll admit. Startling in just how eager she is for the demise of the Dukovskayas. Of course she's compromised now. She knows there's the chance we will expose her just as Georgi has promised. But it's not her own neck that she's worried about, it's mine. Ours. She wants us dead, Marina and me. Marina, me and Svetlana's variation.

We know that because the moment Georgi hung up the phone, he launched the voice activation software. As primitive as the output is, the scope of the program is exceptional. It traced the next call from Anna's phone and recorded the whole conversation. Like the transcript with the botched Rublevskoye biker, this one was a challenge to comprehend. Gosha listened to it, rapt. He had been pleased with my plan. But he was delighted with Anna Arkhipova's desperate next move.

"Oh dear Lord, this is my favorite part," he said, playing back Anna's directives to Ivan, a dumb tough who doesn't know *Rusalka* from Rasputin but answered, nonetheless: "*Tak tochno,* Anna Dmitrievna, I'll take care of it."

"Go on," begged Gosha, "listen." He handed me the laptop and earphones and I hit PLAY. The cyborg's monotone asked: *Perhaps you are familiar with the bally*

*by balance sheen. It's laughter on tenth have venue. Yes.
That's the best venue in deed.*

Gosha cracked up, but I didn't laugh.

The voice recognition was shit, again. The name of
the ballet by Balanchine is *Slaughter on Tenth Avenue.*
Not *laughter.* Not *manslaughter.* Just slaughter. And the
plot of that particular ballet? A jealous dancer hires a
gunman to kill her rival at the end of a performance.
And so I have a date. With Anna. At the theater. And
after the performance tonight, I have no doubt, with the
stage door on Tenth Avenue.

Here's a brief lesson in Balanchine, from a dancer who
could really take him or leave him: *Slaughter on Tenth
Avenue* ends with the dancer continuing to dance until
the cops nab the bad guys. But the music is all happy-
go-lucky Broadway crap—light-years from Stravinsky's
forest. And like Roma's mother said, most ballets are
just fairy tales.

Now I'm outside, sitting on the benches that old men
warmed yesterday evening. The morning smells . . . different. Expectant. I'm wearing Benjamin Frame's flannel
shirt and waiting for him to arrive with my freshly laun-
dered costume. Panic sweat—there was a lot of that
yesterday. I wonder if my costume will smell like the
morning. Clean but not clear.

I close my eyes and watch the sun make shadows on
my eyelids. My mind wanders, floats somewhere nearby. I
hear birdsong. Not tentative anymore but full-throated.
I wonder if it will be a hot day. I summon a heat wave, and
the red-and-black figures before my eyes begin to dance.

I feel Roma take a seat next to me.

"You okay?"

"Yup." We sit for a moment like that. Then I open my eyes and turn to face him. "My father is on his way."

He nods.

"He wants to take us to lunch. Then I'll go to the theater and he'll go to the airport to get Marina."

"So she's definitely on the plane."

"Just confirmed."

He takes my hand, then reconsiders. It's not my hand he wants. He reaches up and puts his palm to my cheek.

"She's not like you, is she?"

"No. She's not. She's not like anyone."

"Will she do this?" he asks. "I mean, will she be able to do this? She's not going to freak out?"

"I don't think so. Ben will explain it to her. And then she will be brilliant. She may not be a diva, but she's a performer, after all."

"It's an awful lot of explaining to do," he says. "Especially for them."

"They talked for over an hour last night," I answer. "They have a head start." I think actually it was two hours. Roma had already fallen asleep when I crept to the top of the stairs and listened. Benjamin's contribution was a quiet loop of assurance: *Yes, it's late. No, I'm not tired. She's absolutely gorgeous. She's wonderful. She's upstairs in my old room. You remember. Yes, I moved back in when my parents moved to Florida. She's wonderful. Yes, sleeping. Yes, it's late. No, I'm not tired. How are you? She's wonderful, Marya, just wonderful. I saw her dance. Does she have good taste in music, too?*

Now Benjamin pulls up in a beat-up Volvo. I stand, but Roma pulls me back to the bench. He takes my face again, this time in both his hands. It's not even my face he wants now, though. He wants my lips. They're his.

"Coming?" I ask when he lets me.

He shakes his head. "You go. Call me when you are ready and I'll take you into Manhattan."

I start to ask but he's already answering. "I need to arrange for Gosha's protection, too. She's not stupid, Lana. She's made more calls. She wants Gosha dead right after you."

I put my hand over my mouth. How could I have missed this? He sees the alarm in my eyes.

"But it's okay. It's okay. Because the guys she called . . ."

"They're Gosha's guys," I finish for him.

"Exactly. But I need an hour or two. Line things up. I don't want to take any chances—she might find a B team—some Albanians or those nut-job Hasids who whack their own. Maybe she's flying somebody in on the same flight as your mom. Who knows?"

I kick the ground. *Is this stupid? Is this a* skazka? A fairy tale?

"Lana," he says. "This is going to work. Once you leave Brooklyn you will never leave our sight. You will never be in danger. Remember that. Nothing is going to happen to you or to your mother."

"Or to Nina."

"Or to Nina."

"Okay," I say. "Go."

Roma kisses me once more—long enough to bring back the heat wave. Then he pulls on his helmet and I spin south to my father's car.

"How is Georgi?" asks Benjamin as I open the passenger door.

"No harm, no foul," I pronounce in English. It strikes me as the correct answer. From my father's bemused shake of the head, I'm guessing I'm right.

MY FATHER IS PULLING into the parking lot of a restaurant near the marina when I tell him I can't possibly eat.

"Fair enough," he says. "I can't say I have much of an appetite, either."

"Nerves?" I ask.

"And how."

We sit, wondering how to fill this space. It is waiting space.

"Tell me again what's the worst thing that can happen?" he says.

"I'll never dance with the Bolshoi again."

"And the best thing?" he says more nervously.

I take a deep breath. "I'll never dance with the Bolshoi again."

He nods. "I can see the merit then, in this plan."

I'm silent. My mind is on Tenth Avenue and the dance I've set in motion. I feel a scream rising. I stifle it. I yawn.

"I'll be right back," says Benjamin, opening the door. He returns in five minutes, holding two large

Styrofoam cups with straws sticking out of the tops. I think of Nina and the smoothies we shared and wonder if I'm going to be sick.

"You don't have to be hungry to drink a milkshake," he says, handing me one.

I take a sip. It's perfect.

"Come on," he says. "Let's go to the boardwalk."

It's a warm, warm wind that ruffles my hair as we climb the stairs to the wide esplanade. The boardwalk is the speckled brown of old wood soaked with rain and drying quickly. Ahead of us is the beach, with a few impatient sunbathers already claiming the sun.

"The Brighton Beach boardwalk," I say out loud. "Before I left, Ma told me to dance on it."

"Your mother loved the boardwalk. We used to walk from her place down to the amusement park." He turns to the right and jerks his head—*that way*. "Coney Island in the off-season is a specific kind of meditation. Does the unsettled soul good."

I study his profile. I see, as did Roma, a man who is alone, but not lonely. A man at peace. He's looking ahead, at the skeleton of a dormant roller coaster on the horizon.

"That's Coney Island?" I ask.

"That's it. It will open next weekend and show a whole different side of itself. Your mother's favorite spot was about halfway between here and there. Where she could see but not hear the roller coaster. It had meaning for her. It was symbolic, you know?"

I nod. You rise, you fall. I know exactly.

But I'm wrong. That's not what he means.

"It was a landmark in one of her . . . visions," he explains. "She had this dream that one day her mother would appear beneath its ridge and would dance her way down the boardwalk. She dreamt they would be reunited here."

I turn and look at him, but he's looking toward the spot of a dream that did not come true.

I close my eyes. The silhouette of the coaster is burned on the back of my eyelids. I squeeze them harder until flashes of light jump from the corners. They drift across my vision like fireflies. Like a line of jets breaking through low-hanging clouds to land in safety.

"I think her vision was real," I say. "I think she saw the future."

I think that all those years ago, Marina really did foresee a mother joining her daughter after a long absence. An absence more emotional than physical.

I think she saw herself. I think she saw me

ACT FOUR
FIN DU SPECTACLE
MANHATTAN

SIXTEEN
SLAUGHTER ON TENTH AVENUE

Boris Makarov is a bulldog of a cop. His shoulders are three times wider than his hips, his back ripples with muscle, and I swear to God he has a lower tooth that doesn't quite fit under his lip. When he sees me at the counter on Nina's floor in Roosevelt Hospital, he saunters over on legs that want nothing to do with each other.

"You are Lana," he says simply.

"*Da*, I'm Lana."

"She's fine," he says to the nurse at the desk. "Come on," he says to me.

Nina is less responsive to my appearance.

Her breathing is shallow. Her body panting just on the safe side of systemic failure. She's surrounded by monitors, they beep a steady gentle encouragement at her: *stay on this side, the safe side.*

"She only just came off the respirator," says Sergeant Makarov.

I watch her, steeling myself with the knowledge that it was Anna Arkhipova who did this. And that whatever happens, she cannot get away with it. This is not just about my principles: my stubborn insistence on fair play, fair treatment, fair rules. This is a crime. An attempted murder. There are no rules. Arkhipova is fair game.

If that means taking a risk, I'll take it.

When Nina's eyes flutter and then snap open, I nearly cry out. They're so bright, too bright.

"Lana."

I rush to her side and bury my head in the thin sheet.

"Lana," she says again.

"*Da milaya*. It's me, love."

"Anna did this."

"I know," I breathe, gripping her hot hand in mine.

"Is this what it means?" She licks her lips once. "To be the Chosen One?"

I scoot closer to her ear and whisper: "No, Ninochka. I will show you what it means to be the Chosen One. And when I do, we will never dance against death again."

MAKAROV WALKS ME TO the exit. "Follow me," he says, "I wanna show you something."

I follow him out onto Tenth Avenue. The backside of Lincoln Center is just five blocks north. We walk three of them and stop. He stands in the middle of the side-walk and asks, "What do you see?"

On the corner is a four-man street crew wielding jack-hammers. There's a cherry picker farther up the street, ostensibly the phone company but I have my doubts: these are all Gosha's guys.

"Every one of them's armed," says Sergeant Makarov.

The back of my neck tingles. My pulse makes itself felt.

Now the cop raises both eyes skyward without moving his enormous skull. I follow them to a platform suspended several stories in the air. It tilts slightly under the shifting weight of a pair of window washers.

"Please tell me those aren't sharpshooters," I say.

"Nope. Window cleaners. But there are surveillance cameras on their basket, trained right down at the street."

I look back to the street level. They are positioned across from the stage door. That's my mark. It should be easy to hit it, it's half a block long after all, a wider mark than any I'll ever find onstage. But still, it feels like highly risky choreography.

"I gotta get back," he says. "Don't think about it anymore. These guys are professionals."

"Professional what?" I ask.

"They've got good aim," is all he says.

THE DRESSING ROOM FALLS quiet when I enter. Dancers scatter like water droplets from my oily presence. Motionless in their midst is Anna Dmitrievna Arkhipova. She wears an emerald-green dress the color of vengeance. She waits a beat to show me the ice in her eyes, and then she opens her arms wide. "Lana, *milaya*, there you are!"

She embraces me. She smells of French perfume and fear.

"Such a circus it has been without you! The press completely lost their heads. You are quite the sensation! The critics simply adore you and the tabloids have decided to rip you to shreds. Welcome to fame!"

Her laugh is heavy lifting, but she gives it her all.

The girls are watching silently. Dancers are a superstitious bunch. The general belief is that for a good performance, everything should go to hell just before curtain. But there is no precedent for this crazy preamble: a rogue soloist, a false accusation, and now a bullshit welcome. What on earth do you make of that? *My God, how well they wear their masks*, I think. It's a skill I never learned. But I'm a quick study. And everything is riding on my mask.

"Now I've more or less got things calmed down," Anna continues. "I explained to the authorities that you have had an awful lot on your plate with your mother under investigation. They've given me their word that they will leave you alone until tomorrow, when, of course, you will have to go in for questioning."

I feign puzzlement. "For questioning?"

"Well, of course, Lana. There's only so much I can do. You will have to answer for your erratic behavior, dear. For the company you keep. For that strange note you left poor Nina."

"Of course." I suck in my breath. *Careful. Let her dance.* She's the one with two roles. She's the one with one too many pretenses. *Let her trip, but not just yet.* Meanwhile, I keep my footing.

"Yes, of course," I murmur. "I'm sorry I was out of touch, Anna Dmitrievna. I lost my phone."

She doesn't acknowledge our shared lie.

"Imagine, girls . . . it turns out that Lana has relatives here in New York. An uncle, isn't that right, Lana?"

"My father," I say. "A *dyadya* and also my father."

Every girl in the room snaps her head. I don't know what they have heard, my confession or my defiance. They've heard me tell Anna that my truth is bigger than hers. They've heard me announce that I didn't just come here to dance. I came to discover.

I see six pairs of eyes light up with a long-missing fire. I feel the slight shift in energy, the palpable contraction as they draw closer. I have allies. I have a corps. I have a vanguard.

Anna puts a hand on her hip and wags her finger at me playfully. "A family reunion. Leaving me to do damage control until the wee hours. Oh, Lana, the scandalous things they said about your mother. And Ninochka, of course, helping not at all. Girls, honestly, repeat after me . . ." She turns to the room. "No more Jamba Juice! Not ever!"

She's overstepped. The girls, already shifting alliances, send signals.

"*Pozor*, Anna Dmitrievna," hisses Larisa. "Have some decency."

"Decency," Anna snaps back, "will do that girl no good. Only a lawsuit. And believe me, that is what the Bolshoi will deliver. The things they put in their juices here. Their energy boosters and their antioxidants. This is what happens when you allow business schemes and organic trends to replace proper state control and regulation. This is the price of the American obsession with supplements!"

The room is silent. Arkhipova seems to be coming unhinged.

"*Nu chto vy,* Anna Dmitrievna? What the hell?" murmurs Larisa. She gathers up her things and pushes past our deputy director. At the doorway she stops and looks me in the eye. "Good luck, Lana." She uses the traditional Russian expression: *not the down and not the feathers*. The one that dates back to our ancient pagans, for whom a successful spring hunt meant bagging not just the remains . . . but the whole, warm corpse of their prey.

Not that I took her literally. But I answer her with the traditional response: *K chortu.* "To the devil." And I mean it almost literally.

NOW IT'S 6:35. TWENTY-FIVE minutes to curtain. My solo comes at the end of Act One. I'm warmed up, costumed, made up. I've reinforced my shoes with an extra ring of stitches around the box, my hands working fast, my needle a glint. I run my hand over the freshly darned toes. By the end of the night, the stitches will be scars.

I'm gelling my hair into a black cap when Gosha's phone buzzes. I finish the job, I'm sleek as a seal, and I wipe my hands to read Roma's message. Your parents have arrived. I'm treating them to meat on the street. I smile. Insouciance, for the first time since we met at that stupid chicken cart. And this, too: *your parents*. What a strange thing. My delight knows no bounds.

I text back: Tell them I love them. Then I reconsider and don't send. I call. Roma answers.

"Give my mother the phone," I say.

"Allo?"

"Mama. It's me. You okay?"

"I am. I'm okay. And I will see you soon. I can't wait."

"Me neither."

There's a long pause. Neither of us saying that there is so much to be said.

"Okay, then."

"Mama?"

"*Da?*"

"I love you."

"And I love you. Madly."

I hang up the phone and pick up my eye pencil. *Spit on sacrificial maiden*, I think. I draw in the eyes of a warrior.

FORTY-FIVE MINUTES LATER, THERE'S a nebulous carpet in the wings as I bounce on the balls of my toes. It must be a fog machine—Americans love their special effects—but it feels like a crouching challenge. I step over this knee-high shag and head for the box of rosin, where I grind its glittery granules into diamond dust under my shoes. *Shine bright*.

All of the sylphs are tramping offstage. Some of them stop to give me an encouraging kiss. Olga, Tatiana, Elena, Larisa, Sofia, Regina . . . and then Anna.

I'm barely aware of the white noise in the house. The orchestra warming up; the bassoon sounding out the grand hall like a foghorn; the hum of the audience, anticipating a catastrophe. They've seen the news. They've read the program: Lana Dukovskaya, the Chosen One, is back for more.

Where will you stab me now, you bastards?

The orchestra settles into readiness. A faceless phalanx assemble in the wings behind me. They know—my fellow dancers—this Danse Sacrale, loaded with competition and fear, is not to be missed. What I am about to do is not just for sensation. It is for redemption.

A single downbeat propels me onstage, my body in forward motion and my head turned back, still watching for my pursuer. I take slow, halting steps to the center of the stage—*no one will breathe*, I am saying—*no one will breathe easy*. The strings in the orchestra pit flutter like an elevated pulse, and I bounce uneasily on their vibration. The horns and the drums shout threats and I retract my body and soul. I gather all the tension with grasping arms, and then with a single leap, I take possession of the stage. The space between me and the spotlight shrinks, cowed by my reckless turns. I'm spinning madly, racing toward my name and my innocence.

It's only four minutes long, the Danse Sacrale. I have teased it, I have scorned it, I have given it what the audience has come for: Lana, the Chosen One. But now, halfway to its end, I halt. From dead weight, I bend backward and my hands touch my feet. The audience swoons and I give them Svetlana. For the next 120 seconds I revive my grandmother's tragedy. I embrace Svetlana's variation and its desperate game of hide-and-seek, and I wrap it in my own crescendo: a contest of wills; the end of my Bolshoi career; fists raised both in defiance and in victory.

I TAKE THREE CURTAIN calls and rush through a gauntlet of congratulations to the dressing room. Intermission has begun. Arkhipova is waiting.

"Come. We should celebrate," she says without a trace of irony or enthusiasm.

I drape my trench coat over my shoulders and slip my feet, still shod in their pointe shoes, into Tatiana's UGGs. I hate the things, but there's no time; Anna is already halfway down the corridor. I hurry after her, following her into the dark alcove of the exit at the end of the hallway. Double doors and a large laundry cart full of *Sylphides* scenery stand between us and the street, where I have backup. But I'm dizzy with the applause. I'm post-performance. I need to recalibrate. I need her to remind me that the music is over. I need her to confess.

"Wait," I say.

She turns, her face livid.

"One second, please," I say. "I'm winded, Anna Dmitrievna. And I have to prepare myself. For what is coming."

I'm appealing to the old Anna. The one whose days involved stamina. Whose nights involved curtain calls. Whose every success was followed by failure, but who carried on, nevertheless, to succeed again. I'm appealing to the artist, the ballerina. She's momentarily speechless, and I press my advantage.

"Please," I say. "Please share some advice. This could be my last performance if you don't tell me how to handle what's coming."

"What's coming," she repeats in a flat voice.

"There will be reporters out there. I know. And they think I did it," I say. I see her wobble on one sharp heel, momentarily uncertain—as if she, too, has the wrong idea about what will be out there.

I put a hand to my throat and play false modesty: "They think that I am the new Bolshoi prototype: treachery, malice, and flawless technique."

I see her wince. My God, the envy. This woman can't stand for the spotlight to be on me—even the spotlight of accusation. I've landed my knife, and now I twist it.

"They know my history, Anna Dmitrievna. You know my history, too. The Dukovskaya history. We are always chosen and we are always sacrificed, the Dukovskayas. My grandmother, my mother. Now me."

I see the flush of red rise from her décolleté up her neck. The rage conquers her face. I'm sure it will be her eyes next that turn red. A dragon in Aladdin's cave. I step closer. I need her voice to roar.

"You know I didn't do this. You know that you have just danced me to my death. Is that what you want? Have you gotten what you wanted? Another chapter in the Dukovskaya tragedy?"

The truth—that she can't win—is obvious even to her. The only thing she can do is amplify our sad story. Our sacrifice. Our Danse Sacrale. Instead, she claws at it, ripping the truth into shreds that can't be made whole.

"That is exactly what I want," she says, her voice clipped. "I want to make it clear, once and for all, that I see through you all. I see through your beautiful bravery, your sickening martyrdom. You were never chosen; you chose your own destiny. Your grandmother was a traitor, your mother was a deserter. And you, Lana, you are a hider. A secret keeper."

A *secret keeper*. I can play that. "And what secret is that? That the Bolshoi is in the hands of a woman who has poisoned her own dancer out of an old grievance and petty jealousy?"

She steps close to me. The French perfume is gone. The fear is gone. I smell the stench of poison and of fever as she opens her mouth: "You played your part flawlessly, Lana Dukovskaya. You were a perfect Chosen One. You fought me, you ran from me, and now you will keep my secret. Now you will pay for the sins of your elders. I have been waiting for this moment, Lana, since before you were born."

"Will you really let them try me for attempted murder?" I ask. "For poisoning Nina with pills that you brought in your suitcase and dropped in the orange juice that you served her? Is that really how this will end? Don't you have something better?"

That's when she leans against the door, flooding the dark alcove with diffused sunset. "Of course I do," she says as she steps out onto Tenth Avenue, where my mother is waiting to greet me.

"Anya," Marina says, smiling. "You've made my daughter a star."

I'LL NEVER KNOW WHAT it meant, the shock on Anna's face when she stood face-to-face with my mother. Maybe she hadn't really believed that Georgi had beaten her and had managed to spring Marina from prison; maybe she believed him, but hadn't anticipated a physical encounter with the woman whom she had resented and ruined in equal measure. Or maybe Anna was just reacting to a new logistical challenge: two Dukovskayas and only one hit man, and she knew from the botched job on Rublevskoye highway how that could end.

But there's no more time to play mind games, because the whine of a distant engine reminds us that the street is an empty stage and we must stand on our marks.

She grabs my arm and drags me forward as the whine becomes a roar. A lone motorcycle crests the hill south of us and accelerates. She has my forearm in a vise grip and doesn't seem to notice that I have hers. That in this *pas de deux* we are equally committed to holding each other steady. The motorcycle is twenty feet away when I see it—brandished in his left hand, what looks like a gun. Has he really brought a gun?

Don't do it, my brain shrieks, as I remember Sergeant Makarov's cameras trained on us. Anna jerks us both back to the sidewalk and for a split second I'm both relieved and dismayed that she has seen what's about to happen to her. But I'm wrong. She has only changed her mind about one thing. I am not her Chosen One, after all. She abandons me. I watch her seize Marina by her shoulders and heave her mightily into the street.

I scream.

For no good reason.

Because Roma is a man with excellent aim.

He spins on a dime, his wheels kicking the puddles in the gutter. He holds the camera in his left hand steady. He asks Anna Dmitrievna to sit down quietly on the pavement while he calls the police.

Then he turns to my mother.

"I'm so sorry if I've splattered your dress, Marina Viktorovna," he says.

WE DON'T WAIT LONG for the police, of course. They show up quicker than the cops in Balanchine's hammy ballet, though not quite so flamboyantly and in less interesting costumes.

Makarov cuffs Anna himself and leads her to the back of his squad car where she sits quietly, her face turned away from us. The cop lingers long enough to admire the resolution of Roma's handheld first-person witness: Anna Arkhipova deliberately pushing Marina Dukovskaya into the path of a speeding motorcycle.

"Not bad," he grunts. "Not exactly Steadicam, but not bad."

I pull the tape recorder from my jacket pocket and rewind it six minutes. "Not exactly hi-fi," says Makarov, but it, too, tells a sordid story. I start to hand it over as well, but I think better of it. Roma nods when I tuck it back into my pocket. We're both a bit wary of the slipperiness of trust.

"Later," he says. "We don't want to lose that."

Marina is sitting cross-legged on the sidewalk, talking animatedly into Roma's phone. I don't know if it's Benjamin or Gosha who is listening on the other end. My mother's never looked as happy as she does now, retelling the climactic role she has just performed. "Tell you what," I hear her say, "I should get the Prix Benois for that one."

She should, I think, as I watch this woman who is transformed, slowly becoming whole to me. She should get the gold prize. She should get all the prizes and all the stolen gold, not just the gold spilling down the back of the theater, the reflection of a sun setting in freshly washed windows, four stories above street level. She laughs. Laughter on Tenth Avenue.

I watch the squad car pull away, lights flashing without sound, followed by a convoy of news vans. The Bolshoi Ballet gets another international news cycle.

"Come on," I say, grabbing Roma by the elbow and scooping up my mother, "I'm not ready for a pack of reporters."

Back inside the theater, the troupe is churning toward Act Two, unaware of the drama outside. They are already onstage, in position for a selection of variations I didn't even know was on the program. Roma finds us an empty practice room to wait it out until the performance is over and the chips begin to fall. But

Marina doesn't want to hide out backstage. She wants to watch the *Corsaire* variation and no one's going to stop her.

"I'll find my way." She smiles. She is on the phone again as she heads into the maze of Lincoln Center backstage. "Ben—come on, just find some secret passage! You know this place better than me . . . Come on, live a little. Meet me stage left."

She turns and blows me a kiss. I shake my head, baffled but pleased.

"I suppose I should call Gosha," I say to Roma, who is lounging comfortably on a ratty couch, his feet propped up on one end, his head cradled in the hammock of his laced fingers.

"Yep," he agrees.

"I suppose I should find Evgeniy Kondratyev. He's technically the press secretary of the ballet. He'll have to do his job for the first time ever in about an hour, now that Anna is being booked down at the precinct house. She won't be taking questions, that's for sure."

"Only from the judge," agrees Roma.

But still I don't move. There's time for that. These things will come on their own: the reporters, the statements, the depositions, the trial.

I bend down and take off Tatiana's hideous UGGs to reveal my own shoes underneath. They've served me well. I hear the distinctive cadence of an audience greeting the conductor. Act Two has begun. Then the rich accents of the next piece. It sounds like Prokofiev.

"Prokofiev?" I ask my tired feet.

Roma snorts. "*Kakoy zhe* Prokofiev? Lana, shame on you."

I turn. He's smiling at me. The gap in his teeth is the new love of my life. "Rachmaninov, *Opus 39*."

"Ahhh." I nod. "Thank you, music scholar."

He winks. Not a flirty wink. If anything it's lazy. I've never seen this. Roma, off guard, unplugged, done for the day. He drapes an arm over the end of the couch and pulls up with a trumpet. It's Lincoln Center, after all, trumpets hang out in the corners. He examines it, his brow furrowed.

"Anyone can recognize Rachmaninov, Lana." He tsks. "But it's not everyone will tell you that *The Seagull*, a ballet by Boris Eifman, is set to music by Sergei Rachmaninov."

"Yes. Indeed," I agree. "Thank you, ballet scholar."

I sit down on a battered folding chair and begin unlacing my shoes, my eyes on Roma as he examines the trumpet. He pulls the mouthpiece from the horn and polishes it on his shirtsleeve. "Close the door, would you?" he asks. "I think we've had enough Russian music for today."

I cross the room and close the door, which is solid and padded—the practice room is soundproofed. The theater and all of the outside world falls mute. For a moment there is only Roma and me and a trumpet.

Then Gosha's phone joins us from my trench coat.

"*Allo*," I say.

"*Nu*, tell me everything," says Dyadya Gosha. "Let's hear your report."

"Later, Gosh," I say. "Full report later. But it went fine. Arkhipova's in custody. Makarov can give you details. Are you being released tonight? Should we come get you?"

"You know, I'm rather enjoying it here. The delightful food, the solicitous dames . . ." he says. I don't answer. I'm watching Roma running his fingers over the valves of his instrument, licking his lips as an introduction. "Lana. Are you listening? Yes, of course you should come get me, you *poganka*!"

"Okay, Gosh . . . we'll be down tonight. We'll bust you out. You won't spend another night in Coney Island Hospital."

I am teasing Georgi Levshik. It's come to that.

"Okay. But just you and Roma. I don't want Marya seeing me this way. Marya waits until tomorrow."

"It's a deal," I say. I hang up the phone. I pull off one shoe and swing it by its ribbons. Not a wrecking ball, a lasso. I let it fly across the small room and laugh.

Roma gives the trumpet two blasts and then stands from the couch and begins to play. He plays soft and low, backstage. He plays soulfully, tenderly. He plays that most beautiful of songs: George Gershwin's "Summertime."

I remove my other pointe shoe as he plays and put the chair in the corner so that I have room. Then I dance barefoot to Roma's song. Barefoot, like a young pagan, I banish spring and embrace what's next. Summertime.

EPILOGUE
VORKUTA

Summer has only just arrived in Vorkuta. Green grass and birdsong are brand-new above the Arctic Circle, but there's plenty of daylight. The evening performance has just ended and we will walk to the hotel in low sunlight.

I wonder, as I remove the last of my eye makeup and strip off my tights, if the Bolshoi ever came to Vorkuta.

Just as I predicted to my father that day one year ago, I never danced with the Bolshoi again. The weeks after New York were a blur of attorneys, depositions, affidavits and eventually a trial. A sensational trial, full of tear-streaked primas and monosyllabic bookkeepers and bumptious trustees protesting too much. (They were *shocked, shocked* by the sordid goings-on backstage at the ballet. Never would they have turned a blind eye to such abuses of power.)

The new artistic director, Pavel Vartukh's successor,

invited me back for the following season but I declined. Not because I wasn't too sure that this new guy would really be able to "reform and restore the Bolshoi, Russia's crown jewel," as he promised, but because I was sure I wanted to dance on a different stage.

I dance with Dolgorukov now. I'm one of the best in the company but Dolgorukov is progressive and doesn't have a hierarchy. I'm not a "prima" or a "principal," and I will never be an "Artist of the People," and that's fine with me. We are always on the road. I've seen more of Russia than I knew even existed. It's the first year that Dolgorukov has had the funds to tour, and we've barely stopped since they became available four months ago.

Three guesses as to where those funds came from.

I wouldn't have accepted it, of course. Not after dancing my way clear of Dyadya Gosha's tangled strings. I wouldn't accept it if there was a chance that Georgi, unrepentant and proud of the rave reviews that followed my New York debut, would start meddling. But Gosha is dead, and it was his last wish that we use his fortune to restore ballet, both privately and publicly.

We decided together, my mother and I.

"Let Roma have it," I had said initially. "He has big plans for a mixed jazz ensemble—a cooperative between musicians and dancers. One that I would consider joining if it had real prospects. Give it to Roma."

It had been particularly hard on Roma, Gosha's dying. For a while after the tour, he had steered clear of his old boss. He said he needed more time for his music, and the old man didn't argue. But after the stroke, Roma spent a solid week at Georgi's bedside. He felt responsible, of course. It was months after the head injury and doctors said there was no way to connect the two . . . But still, a man dies of a stroke and you have to wonder where that blood clot started. I reminded him that we both attacked him that night, but it didn't help him to share the guilt. My father told me to be gentle with Roma. He knew—a death on your conscience is a heavy burden.

It was both harder and easier when Daniela walked out of the hospital a month after Georgi's death on her own two legs, steady and poised. And when Nina, under oath at the trial, described her certainty that she would be dead if not for Georgi Levshik, who had rescued her from an alleyway behind that terrible hotel.

But even though I had—we all had—managed to live and learn, to forgive and forget, I was wary of the money. It was Marina who convinced me. She said that it was up to Roma and me to make it clean. To redeem Gosha.

SO I TOOK THE money and took Dolgorukov on tour.

We travel by train, falling asleep in birch forests and waking in the tundra. In addition to Vorkuta, we have traveled to Oryol, Perm, and as far as Magadan.

"They should call it the Gulag tour," laughs Nina.

Yes, she came, too.

She signed up the day after I did. "I'm up for anything," she had said. "Anything except fresh-squeezed juice."

Nina and the others have already changed and rushed out to get something to eat before the buffet closes. I'm waiting behind because I want to call Marina in private. It's my birthday. I always congratulate my mother on my birthday. It seems only fair.

I check the clock and dial the number. Once again, it is busy. It doesn't worry me anymore, a busy signal on Marina's phone. Nine times out of ten it means she's talking long distance. She and Benjamin Frame spend more time talking on the phone than most teenagers I know. I guess because they don't text.

I put the phone down and glance around at this makeshift dressing room in a cavernous hall still called a Miner's Palace of Culture. Vorkuta, once a hub of the Gulag, the Soviet Union's penal colony, is just one in a string of towns that, though they are no longer the "secret cities" they were in the last century, have been kept in the dark about the secret of Russia's twenty-first-century wealth and power. They are grim, these hinterland ghost towns. Industrial wastelands, former prison camps, closed research zones where little is researched anymore but poverty, alcoholism and abandoned hopes. But between them stretches all of Russia. And when I dance, I dance for an audience that is not just starved for ballet . . . it is appreciative.

I stuff my tights into my bag and pull on my jeans. I'm toweling some of the gel out of my shellacked hair when there's a light knock on the door. I see her in the mirror before I can turn and greet her—an old woman with long grey hair pulled back into a loose braid. Her face is weary. It is the face of a much-tested life. Deep circles pillow dulled blue eyes. Deeper lines run maps on her face. Yet she stands upright, unbent. With the posture of a much younger woman. With the posture, I realize, of a dancer.

Dobriy vecher, she says shyly. Her smile is brief, subversive, as though she doesn't want anyone to catch it.

"Good evening."

She says nothing more, just wrings her hands and casts her gaze around the room and its sparse remnants of our performance.

"It was very exciting," she finally says.

I pull out a chair and gesture for her to sit. She walks slowly toward it, but before she gets to it, an officious young girl enters the room behind her.

"Now, *babushka*, didn't I tell you—the dancers don't have time to prattle with you about ballet. They have dinner to get and a schedule to keep. Come now, off with you."

The girl takes the old woman's elbow and begins to lead her away, still talking over her shoulder.

"Terribly sorry. Some of our old folks are . . . well, a bit, you know. They've had a hard life and they, some of them, have these delusions." She drops her voice and rolls her eyes a bit. "This one spent too much time in the *psikhushka* psych ward. Thinks she's a prima ballerina."

They are nearly in the hallway when I find my voice.

"Stop. Please bring her back. Let her stay."

They turn and look at me.

"I know her," I say.

The girl's face is puzzled. Svetlana Dukovskaya's is not.

GLOSSARY OF RUSSIAN WORDS:

apteka—pharmacy

babushka—grandmother or more generally, old woman

baryshnya—young lady, gentility

bozhe—exclamation. God!

chort—exclamation. Devil.

chto sluchilos'—what happened?

da—yes

dacha—dacha, country house

derzhis'—hold on

devushka—girl

dobriy vecher—good evening, a greeting

dorogaya—my dear

dyadya—uncle

fortochka—small window

gastronom—grocery store

glasnost—openness, refers to a state policy of more government honesty adopted by Soviet authorities in the 1980s

grib—mushroom

Gulag—the network of Russian prison camps

k chortu—exclamation. To the devil! Used in response to a well-wisher before a performance

kak ona pogibla—how did she die?

kak ona pokonchila soboy—how did she kill herself?

kak ona umerla—how did she die?

kak zvali tvoyu mamu—what was your mama's name?

knizhniy—bookstore

krasivaya—pretty

milaya—sweetheart, my sweet

mukhomor—type of poisonous mushroom

nemedlenno—immediately

ne nashla—I didn't find

ne tak—not that way

nochnoy klub—night club

nu—well?

po-angliyski—in English

polniy bred—ravings, delirium

poshli—let's go

pozor—exclamation. Shame!

psikhushka—slang for psychiatric hospital

rebyata—guys, friends

seychas—coming now

skandaly—scandals

skazhite pozhaluysta—tell us please

skazka—fairytale

slova—words

Sovok—slang term for Soviet, an "everyman" of the Soviet Union

spasibo—thank you

spokoyno—easy, go easy

stariki—old men

tvoya mama—your mama

tyotya—aunt

ubili—they killed

vazhnaya persona—VIP

vecher—evening

vecherinka—party

vot—there

vremenno nidostupen—temporarily unavailable

vzglyadi—glances, looks, gazes

zdes—here

zhopa—slang for rear end, ass

AUTHOR'S NOTE

Hider, Seeker, Secret Keeper is a work of fiction. Any resemblance to individuals, living or dead, is unintentional. Or more honestly, rather unavoidable. Let me explain:

The Bolshoi Ballet, as one of the world's oldest ballet companies, presents a writer with nearly 250 years' worth of lore for inspiration. Recently, the stories out of the famous theater have been more lurid than lovely: high-profile defections, smear campaigns, allegations of corruption, bribery, and worse crimes—these are some of the Bolshoi headlines not found in the "Arts" section.

Every ballet company in the world has its intrigue and scandals. But when, on a cold Moscow night in January 2013, a masked assailant threw a jar of sulfuric acid into the face of the Bolshoi Ballet's young artistic director, Russia's renowned theater entered into an unprecedented year of relentless drama. For months violence, vengeance, and an air of siege reigned. The protracted scandal grew worse, taking more victims with each development: the director blinded, the theater's executive director sacked, a revered Artist of the People terminated, a rising star hounded from the stage, and a principal dancer—still proclaiming his innocence—sentenced to six years in a "strict regime" prison.

It was during this annus horribilis that I began writing this sequel to *Dancer, Daughter, Traitor, Spy* with this question in mind: What happens when your greatest dream—joining the Bolshoi Ballet—becomes a nightmare?

Elizabeth Kiem
Brooklyn, March 2014

ACKNOWLEDGMENTS

Thanks to Dan, my cheerleader; Nancy, my coach; Sunita for all the Hail Marys; and Joy, my phantom touchdown. With apologies for the sports metaphors.

Continue reading for a preview of

ORPHAN, AGENT, PRIMA, PAWN

PROLOGUE
VORKUTA 2015

In a dimly lit dressing room in a dank Siberian theater in the twilight of an Arctic summer, Lana Dukovskaya marvels at the speed with which the answer to one question can reveal so many others.

For eighteen years, she peered through a veil of secrets. Then, in the short span of a spring week, this was revealed: her inscrutable mother, her anonymous father, and the thing that came between them—the woman sitting silently before her now, a grandmother who disappeared before Lana was born.

Almost overnight, Lana had gained a family. And she inherited all its secrets.

Now it is time to unpack that inheritance. Whether by fate or coincidence, Lana's traveling dance troupe has brought her to the doorstep of Svetlana Dukovskaya—a former prima ballerina of the Bolshoi Ballet, a fallen Artist of the People. Lana feels the veil strain under her fingers, as if she might rip it in half. But she is about to learn that her family's secrets did not begin with Svetlana Dukovskaya; they are older and deeper than she had imagined.

"*You have a daughter named Marina,*" *she says, taking the old woman's hand. She feels paper-thin skin, knuckles locked stiff, and an uncertain pulse at the wrist. She searches the heavily lined face for familiar features, calculating quickly. Her grandmother would be close to seventy years old.*

"*Marina is my mother,*" *she continues.* "*Do you remember her, your daughter? Do you remember Marina?*"

The old woman turns away. Lana watches her face drain of expression and imagines the worst—that this chance encounter has come too late. That the years of imprisonment, psychiatric treatment, and abandonment have stolen too much and that her grandmother has forgotten everything—even the stage. It is the same stage upon which Lana and her mother Marina both danced. But neither of them made the stage of the Bolshoi Theatre a throne, as Svetlana Dukovskaya had.

Until she was removed from it.

Lana probes gently: "*I danced with the Bolshoi once, too. Before I joined the troupe that you saw tonight, I was in the corps of the Bolshoi Ballet.*"

The old woman's eyes dart around the dressing room. A portrait of the president—shrewd and reptilian, not a fan of the ballet—hangs on a water-stained wall. Next to it, a closet stands open, its door sags on a busted hinge. Underneath the closet is a dusty runner with a hammer and sickle motif. The dressing room has not known a decorative thought in thirty years.

Her grandmother's gaze lands on the mirror before

them. Lana asks, "Do you remember dancing with the Bolshoi?"

"Of course I do."

Her voice is louder than Lana expected.

"I remember everything."

Svetlana Dukovskaya peers into the mirror as if searching for something beyond its reflection. She taps the glass with one finger and says, "I am nothing but memories. Memories that aren't even mine . . . I am a rememberer."

She closes her eyes, but they are not still. Lana can see them dance under age-spotted lids. She can see the memories ripple across her grandmother's brow and tremble on colorless lashes. When they open once more, Svetlana Dukovskaya's eyes are bright. She turns from the mirror and raises both hands, light and pale as lunar moths, to touch her granddaughter's cheeks.

"Dochka," she murmurs—the word that can mean daughter or, simply, a girl too young to know better. Then she corrects herself: "Granddaughter."

"Shall I tell you what I remember, granddaughter?"

ACT ONE: ORPHAN
MOSCOW, 1958-1959

ONE
POX

It was a strange coincidence, the news coming on the same day: there was smallpox in Moscow, and my mother was back in town.

We'd heard about the quarantine in the morning: *Restricted civilian movement until otherwise reversed by the Protectorate of Moscow Region Health Inspectorate and Population Control as ordered by the Ministry of Health, USSR.* So by dinnertime, when Matron took me aside to tell me that my mother had been released, there was no way to know if that meant I would see her in a matter of days, or of weeks.

I wasn't sure which I preferred.

Of course it was possible I wouldn't see her at all. She didn't have to come looking for me. My mother had been gone eight years, and in all that time her name was unmentionable. Not since I was seven years old had I heard it pronounced. When Matron said it aloud, it sounded every bit as archaic and unlikely as "the pox."

"Vera Konstantinovna Kravshina has been released," is what she said. "It is her right, as a rehabilitated citizen, to reclaim you from the state's ward. Because you are not yet of legal age, Svetlana, you have no input in the matter. If anyone is going to deny your mother's petition, it will be me."

I could smell dinner being prepared in the kitchen at the end of the corridor. The smog of stuffed cabbage was as familiar as the tang of old books and wet wool, but for years afterward the smell would cause me a moment of panic. A moment when I felt I was about to be thrown to the wolves.

"Do you understand, Svetlana? It is entirely my decision whether you rejoin your mother and her compromised history or you stay here with us, in the House. The matter is in my hands."

But she was wrong, Matron was. It was not entirely in her hands and neither was I. There were others making the decisions. I just didn't know it yet. Just like I didn't know for sure who was the wolf.

LATER THAT AFTERNOON, IN the courtyard with Oksana, I repeated Matron's words about my leaving the House.

"A pox on both your houses!" Oksana retorted.

It was her favorite new curse. Our teacher, Lydia Timofeevna, had passed out the scenes from *Romeo and Juliet* the week before the smallpox outbreak. Most teachers in the tenth class assigned stories about handsome farmers, clever shepherdesses, and brave soldiers; tales full of burbling streams and birch trees. In these stories there was plenty of collective achievement securing the glory of the Motherland . . . but no teen sex. No duels. No angry curses on aristocrats.

But Lydia Timofeevna had ignored the Soviet Ministry of Education's standard fare and handed us a soap opera from Verona.

"Shakespeare, boys and girls, was an English imperialist dog," she declared. "But he was a dog with perfect pentameter, razor-sharp satire, and the barbed tongue of a true class warrior. And that, children, is something to make note of."

Oksana had made note. She had memorized whole passages, sharpening her barbed tongue. She even dug up the original and mined it for its most peculiar Shakespearean phrases, which she then taught to me. I was a poor student, but in memorizing one simple phrase: "I do bite my thumb, good sir," I effectively doubled my primitive English vocabulary.

When Matron posted the STATEMENT OF QUARANTINE AS PERTAINING TO ALL MUNICIPAL HOUSING BLOCKS in the meeting room, Oksana greeted it as Mercutio would: "A pox on both your houses!"

Which meant, of course, a pox on *our* House.

There was only one House for me and Oksana. It was a pale yellow four-story brick of a building on the end of a quiet street that curved with the river. There were other houses on the street—squat piles from the last century in various states of dilapidation—but there was only one House. The sign on the gate identified it: THE HOUSE FOR ORPHANED CHILDREN, #36. It was no secret what kind of orphans we were—solo not because of death or

abandonment, but because our parents were political sui-
cides. Orphanage #36 was exclusively for the children of
Enemies of the People. It had been my home for more
than half my life.

By then, eight years seemed like a long time to stay put
in one house. In our Soviet Union, the authorities were
always plucking citizens from their beds and rearranging
them according to some mysterious political calculus. I
sometimes wondered how many times my mother had
changed beds, stared at new walls, made new neighbors.
I knew from her letters that she had passed through at
least three different prison camps, maybe in three different time zones.

Enemies of the People pay for their crimes with hard
labor and countless kilometers.

But by the autumn of 1958, they were making the
long trip back. Comrade Stalin was gone, and the new
leader had called for an era of forgiveness. Hundreds of
thousands of prisoners were released from the prison
Gulag, my mother among them. We had seen them, the
lost souls turning up on the train platforms of Moscow
looking like ghosts from a darker time. They didn't look
forgiven. Forgotten, maybe. But even that wasn't really
true. We had only pretended to forget. About Stalin and
the nights when our neighbors were dragged away in
their pajamas. About the photographs we burned and
the letters we hid. About the time when they asked us if
we had ever heard our parents whispering, and we nodded, once: *yes*.

Anyway, it made no difference. Whether they had

been pardoned by the State or forgiven by the People, it didn't change who *we* were: We were, and always would be, the children of Enemies of the People. We were wards of Orphanage #36. We were tainted.

A pox on our House, indeed.

OKSANA HANDED ME THE ping-pong ball and propped up the sagging net with a twig. A gust of wind blew a fresh shower of leaves into the courtyard. November nibbled at my fingers as I bounced the ball on the dilapidated table. She said, "The busses are still running. In theory your mother could show up any minute."

I made a spastic serve and she went to fetch the ball. On the other side of the brick wall, the antennae of a passing trolleybus sparked against the electric cables hanging over the street.

"Is it the number twelve?" I asked.

The #12 trolley left from Kursky Station. It was the bus that my mother would take if she were coming to the House.

"Fie, 'tis no number twelve," said Oksana, now the bard of public transport. "That fine beast is a noble stag cut loose from a primordial wood."

"And I suppose you will be comparing it to a summer day?"

We were both at the gate now. Oksana looked out. I didn't. There was no way I was going to star in some maudlin scene: anxious mother, pale-faced daughter, hands gripping iron bars, tearful reunion. All forgiven. All forgotten.

But Oksana said, "Look," so I did. A woman was climbing off the bus at our stop.

"Is it her?" whispered Oksana.

The bus pulled away. The woman's face was hidden. She had bent over to rearrange the contents of her shopping bags. I noticed her stocking, which had slid below her knee. I noticed a dried brown leaf that had fastened itself to her coat sleeve. There was nothing else to notice. She was a lady with baggage. She could have been thirty or a hundred and thirty. She could have come from the Gulag or from the other side of town. I had no idea if she was my mother.

"Is it her?" Oksana said again.

The woman lifted the bags. She was crossing the street, facing us, closing the gap. In a moment she would be at the gate, and now I noticed everything: the slight limp, the thin lips, the fatigue, and the impatience. I noticed carrot greens sprouting from one of the net bags. The woman glanced at the plaque on the gate and halted. She looked me full in the face. Then, the woman who was not my mother spat deliberately on the ground and kept walking.

"Parasites," we heard her mutter.

A single potato dropped from one of her net bags and rolled toward us. Oksana lunged through the gate and grabbed it. She hurled it at the woman's back. She missed.

"It doesn't matter," she said, slipping an arm around my waist. "In a matter of months we will be sixteen. Old enough to go wherever we want. Neither Matron nor your mother will have any claim on you. We'll pack a bag of liverwurst and gingerbread and set out for the Altai, just like the sleeping twins of the Phoenix Plains."

I didn't answer. I had never heard of the sleeping twins of the Phoenix Plains, but I loved that they wandered somewhere in Oksana's clever head. Still, I knew that was not our fate—a life of vagabond gingerbread. Our fate was to be a number in a ledger of Orphanage #36. We might soon be free of its walls, but we would never be free of its stigma. Even far away in the Altai.

Unless.

"Unless what?"

I hadn't meant to say it out loud.

"Unless what, Svet? Unless your mother makes you go live with her in some barrack halfway house for the officially pardoned outcasts of the Gulag?"

"No." I shook my head. My idea of escape was wilder than an official pardon, and Oksana knew it.

"Oh, right," she said. She stooped to pluck the ping-pong ball from the weeds. "I forgot. There's no ballet out on the Phoenix Plains. Guess I'll have to find another twin."

I had only been studying ballet for four years. But I knew I was good. Really good. Just last week I reached a new level: a triple pirouette level; a sustained 120-degree side extension level; a level of musical and physical connection that had, at its hot core, an epiphany. *This. This would save me. Ballet would be my ticket. My exit.* I blazed through that lesson like a fire. I was no nomad of the Phoenix Plains—I, myself, was the phoenix, the firebird.

Sure enough, at the end of the lesson, Elena Mikhailovna had kept me back to tell me that if I continued to progress through the winter, she would recommend me for the Bolshoi Academy in the spring. Since then, my hazy horizon was crystal clear. No mirage on some fairy-tale plain.

"I have a chance," I said. "The only chance I will ever have."

"All right then," Oksana said, her face serious. "I'll stay, too. I'll stay right here in Moscow. And when you get cast as Juliet at the Bolshoi Ballet, I'll be your Mercutio."

I laughed. *Romeo and Juliet* might be ideologically suspect as a play, but as a ballet, it was the sensation of the season. As long as the bourgeois lovers were silent and choreographed by Communists, the Soviet Ministry of Culture approved of their star-crossed plight. Even celebrated it. Especially if Galina Ulanova, the Bolshoi's leading lady, danced the role of Juliet.

"I'm not sure Ulanova will approve of your plan," I said.

"Ulanova!" cackled Oksana. "She's forty years old, Sveta! You do realize that Juliet is supposed to be fourteen? Now please tell me how Galina Ulanova, fabulous as she may be, can pretend to be a fourte-year-old virgin?"

"Ulanova's unsurpassed technical maturity brings depth to an emotionally underdeveloped character," I said, but Oksana just rolled her eyes and gave me a look that said: *balls*.

"Besides," I said, "Juliet loses her virginity halfway through the story, remember? Why else would she be willing to die for that moony-eyed Romeo?"

Oksana twirled her paddle and wrinkled her nose.

"Well, all I know is that when *you* dance Juliet, nobody will have to praise your 'technical maturity' because *your* Juliet will actually be a teenager. A real teenager with raven hair, a face as fair as the east, and a body the boys die for. Just like Bill-chik, that imperialist hack, intended."

We played until the dark swallowed the ping-pong ball completely. Then we went inside. Another day had passed and we still hadn't caught smallpox. And I still hadn't seen my mother.

"WELL, CLEARLY, THIS OUTBREAK just shows that we have gotten too friendly with India. India's Communist Party apparatus is still unformed and it will never catch up with the Soviet Union in technological, scientific, or medical achievements."

That was Lara V., of course. Lara was a model student. She got excellent marks, wore her hair in perfect plaits, and was the best speaker in Orphanage #36's chapter of the Communist Youth Union, the Komsomol. She also had a beautiful singing voice. I liked Lara all right, but mostly when she was singing.

"That is an informed answer," said Andrei Samoilovich with nasal ambivalence. He tapped his pen on his cheek, a nervous habit that had given our geography teacher a permanent set of inky freckles. "But we cannot state, explicitly, that the outbreak of this ancient disease, which has no place in our highly developed society, necessitates a change in foreign policy. It is, after all, the duty of the Soviet Union to assist all countries trapped in a backward system to further their political and economic growth until they have achieved the same level of socialized harmony and Party unity as the Communist Party of the Soviet Union."

Lara nodded. Oksana stifled a yawn. I wrote the words "Party unity" on my slate and gave them a mustache like Comrade Stalin's. You could do that now. Now that Stalin was dead and his "excesses" exposed, you could make jokes. Like the one about his mustache wandering off his face to snack on the crumbs in his lap. That kind of joke. You could even call the new leader—jolly, bald, gap-toothed Nikita Khrushchev—by silly nicknames: *Nikitinka, Nikitushka, Nikitulka.*

"In this instance, we have to consider the recklessness of the individual who brought this scourge upon us," continued Andrei Samoilovich. "Was it not the fault of the citizen himself? This artist, whose productivity was minimal at best? Was it not his responsibility to be more vigilant while on foreign soil and prevent this terrible biological contagion?"

His beady eyes were roaming. I ducked them. I didn't want to answer the question, though its answer was obvious. The answer was: "Yes, Andrei Samoilovich. It was the comrade-artist's duty to be more vigilant while on foreign soil."

But I felt sorry for the poor bugger who had brought smallpox back from India. He was a ceramicist or something, traveling with a delegation of artists to a conference in Delhi. He died a week after they returned. So did half of his family and an old man who lived in their communal apartment. That's when the posters appeared in the subway and the announcements began on the radio. That's when people began talking disapprovingly about "cultural exchanges" and "folk art."

All I could think about—beyond the horrors of the disease that, according to Rosa D.'s medical textbook, turned your skin to scabs and bled you from the inside out—was how that ceramicist must have felt when he was told: *Your art is exceptional. Your talent will be rewarded. You will represent your country and your people on the world stage!*

What I wouldn't give to hear those words, to be recognized and chosen.

But that's something you didn't admit if you were a good Soviet citizen. You couldn't suggest that you were better, let alone exceptional. And you couldn't be jealous of someone else's achievements, because there's no envy among comrades. A true Soviet knew not to covet good fortune—better to be smug at bad luck. Better to sneer slightly, like Andrei Samoilovich did when he pronounced the word "ceramicist."

I imagined the artist I secretly envied exploring an exotic city, meeting fellow potters from all over the world, buying his wife a silk sari maybe, or lotus tea, and thinking the whole time, *today New Delhi, tomor-row—the world!*

It didn't work out, though, for the poxy potter. Instead, it was *today New Delhi, tomorrow—the grave.*

So when Andrei Samoilovich called my name I just said, "Certainly it was his fault. He's dead, after all."